This book should be returned to any branch of the
Lancashire County Library on or before the date shown

1 0 AUG 2015

0 2 NOV 2015

Arabella Weir is an actress, comedian and writer best known for *The Fast Show*. She makes regular appearances on TV and radio and is a frequent contributor to national newspapers. She has written several books for adults including the international bestseller, *Does My Bum Look Big in This?*, and the Tabitha trilogy for younger readers. She lives in North London with her two teenagers and maybe a dog . . . soon.

The TABITHA trilogy

The Rise and Rise of Tabitha Baird
The Endless Trials of Tabitha Baird
Testing Times for Tabitha Baird

THE
ENDLESS TRIALS
OF TABITHA BAIRD

ARABELLA WEIR

Piccadilly
PRESS

First published in Great Britain in 2015
by Piccadilly Press
Northburgh House, 10 Northburgh Street,
London EC1V 0AT

www.piccadillypress.co.uk

Text copyright © Arabella Weir, 2015
Illustrations © Mina Bach, 2015

A CIP catalogue record for this book
is available from the British Library.

ISBN: 978-1-848-12436-3

1 3 5 7 9 10 8 6 4 2

Typeset by Palimpsest Book Production Limited,
Falkirk, Stirlingshire
Printed and bound by Clays Ltd, St Ives Plc

Piccadilly Press is part of the Bonnier Publishing Group
www.bonnierpublishing.com

To Lilli Fletcher and Luca Ferraro,
my young reader friends,
with much love and huge thanks

AUTUMN TERM WEEK 1

TUESDAY

First day back at school after the summer hols. Super-duper. Golly gosh. So fabulous to be back.

Yeah, right. It is not. I am joking, obvs. I haven't turned into a Grace over the summer holidays! But it is actually totes brill to be back with Emz and A'isha again every day, for the whole day. Yeah, all right, and Grace too. I guess she is part of our gang now, 'officially' as she would say! We all jumped up and down screaming and whooping when we saw each other this morning before the bell. We were so excited to see each other again. Grace didn't whoop and yell, though. I mean, AS IF. She is sort of one of us now, but she hasn't had a brain transplant or anything. She hasn't started copying every single thing we three do, thank god. Anyway, even though she knows she's in with us now, she is still, on purpose, wearing that hairband AND her cardigan done all the way up AND the skirt at the correct length. Must do something about that immediately, otherwise she's out. She can be Grace, but she can't be *a* Grace. I'll have to explain it all to her obvs!

It had been, like, nearly three whole weeks since we were all together, because Emz was away for practically the whole time in Croatia (wherever that is?!) and A'isha's gran had taken the whole family back to where she is originally from. Morocco, I think. A'isha says everyone there is Muslim. A'isha reckoned that in a way it was easier wearing her hijab over there because all the girls and women were wearing them everywhere she went, so she didn't feel so cross about having to wear one too: 'Because there it was just like wearing shoes.' She said she's still working on not wearing it sometime soon, like ASAP. Just as soon as she can get her dad to stop being so obsessed with it. A'isha said now was not the right time, though, because apparently her dad's come back from Morocco extra Messed-up-Muslim because of going to the mosque every day with all his mates over there. She said he never goes over here – weird, isn't it, that people do completely different things in different countries even though they're the same person in both?!

Anyways, guess what? You're not going to guess, obvs – you're a notebook, and last time I checked notebooks can't actually make guesses. Hah, hah. Even though you are a really beautiful new super-special notebook, I will admit. Gran bought it for me, because she'd noticed my old one was a bit tatty. Anyhoo, amazeballs, and not in a good way – it's actually super-bad-amazeballs news. Remember the horrible made-me-sit-on-my-own-in-class-because-she'd-heard-about-me teacher? Yeah, her, Ms Oh-So-Smarty-Pants Cameron. Well, guess what?! She's only been made permanent. She's not a supply any more. She is an actual official teacher at HAC now. So, that is brilliant news. Not. And we had our first period with her, and, of course, being her, she asked if we'd all read the book we were supposed to read over the summer holidays.

Blooming cheek. She stared straight at me while asking this with a full-on sarky face, like she was saying 'Naturally we all know you won't have read it, Tabitha Baird.'

Well, hah-di-hah, have that, Ms Oh-So-Smarty-Pants, I actually did read it and, what's more, I really liked it. Obvs I didn't say that in class in front of everyone though. AS IF. Like I said, I have not turned into a Grace over the summer holidays. I've got a reputation to keep up, especially now that I'm in Year Nine. I can't have people thinking I've gone soft over the summer and somehow magically turned into a Super Nerd. Not looking like a Nerdy Swot is going to be extra important because now that Emz, A'isha and I are actually mates with Grace it's going to be super hard to stop everyone else thinking we've also turned into Nerdy Knicks like her.

Just between us, though, I can tell you that I absolutely lurvvved the book Ms Cameron was sure

I wouldn't have read. And that is pretty amazing because I usually hate reading. I've always hated reading. I never read.

Actually that isn't true any more. It used to be true, but it's not really now. But I don't want Mum to know I've started liking reading, mainly because she'd go and on about how fantastic and brilliant me now liking reading was. So, I'm going to pretend I still hate reading and then just hide whatever book I'm reading from Mum so that she doesn't get all over-excited and hysterical and suddenly think I'm going to be a professor or something now I like reading! I know that might sound a bit random, but I do not want to do things that please her. That is not my job. Duh. I am a teenager and my job is to do things that annoy my mum, not make her happy.

In the days when I actually did hate reading it wasn't my fault anyway. It was Mum's. I hated reading because Mum went on and on and on for as long as I can remember (definitely from when I was too little to be even able to hold up a book, never mind read it!) about how I'd never be an interesting person if I hadn't read mountains of books.

Hmm, funny that, because when Mum isn't writing The Most Boring Blog in the Entire Universe (hers), then she is always reading and she is definitely NOT the most interesting person in the world. Never mind in the world, she's not even the most interesting person in our house!

Of course Luke, my spotty mankenstein little brother thinks he is that person in our house. Yes, all right, it is true, he is apparently, according to his teacher, 'unusually bright'. (I reckon that's actually her code for someone with no mates.) But interesting he is not. How could he be? He plays Scrabble, and I mean actually wants to play it of his own free will, and not because Gran or Mum have said they'll give him chocolate if he plays it with them. I mean, like, he would rather play Scrabble than watch TV. Hello??!!! And as if that weren't bad enough, get this: he 'prefers fruit to chocolate'. Hah! Oh puuuleeze. Or so he claims, although I don't see much evidence of that when it's Christmas and the huge tin of sweets Gran always buys comes out!

Anyway, why am I going on about my nerdy, boring brother? So, at school, it was super brill to see my homies. ('Homies' – do you like that? Cool, isn't it? It means your gang of mates. I don't know why it's 'homies', as in home, though. Weird.) All four of us managed to sit together in practically every class all day long, though obviously not the classes you get streamed for. Grace is, of course, you guessed it, in the top stream for everything that has sets, but that's okay. She's cool. Well, she will be once I've sorted out the hairband, cardigan, skirt length, etc. And it's not like she goes on about being in the top set or anything. She just goes off to her separate classes for whatever and then joins us again afterwards. It's fine.

Oh man, it was great fun seeing the look on people's faces whenever they noticed Grace coming towards our table in class. You could just tell they were thinking

Oh my god, what is she doing?! They're going to be horrible to her! And then when they realised Emz, A'isha and me weren't, but were actually saving a chair for Grace it was brilliant. They didn't know what to think! I admit it is pretty random for us – well, me the most, I suppose – to be friends with Grace, but random is cool. It's great that people still don't know and can't guess how I'm going to be or what I'm going to do. That is the coolest way to be, don't you think?

Oh yeah, nearly forgot – don't know how because you could not miss her – there's a new girl in our class and she is sooo out there. Everything about her is screaming 'notice me': the way she sits, what she wears, the way she speaks, or more like, grunts. She's a goth. Well, I think she is. I mean, she's got jet-black hair (really black, you know, like a plastic bin bag – it's definitely dyed) and wears loads of black eye make-up in huge rings round her eyes. She looks a bit like a panda. And she's got loads of piercings up both her ears – in fact, so many you can't see any of the skin of her earlobes – not that I was looking! But I did notice that one of them, a stud, is a skull, so she is definitely a goth. She must be. Who'd wear a skull earring if they weren't? She didn't talk to anyone as far as I saw and seemed a bit moody and not very chatty – pretty much what you'd expect from a goth, I guess. Apparently her name's Aly, short for Alexandra. So I've thought up a brilliant nickname. I'm going to call her Dark Aly. Hah, hah. Geddit? Dark Aly as in Dark Alley because she's totes goth and scary like a dark alley! That is hilarious. It's so going to catch on. Must tell Emz, A'isha and Grace, although Grace will def not use it. I bet you Grace will think Dark Aly is a mean nickname.

Is it mean? It's not, is it? It's just a joke. Hmm, maybe I'll see what Aly is like before I tell everyone her new nickname. Yes, perhaps that's a nicer thing to do. God, get me, talking about a 'nicer thing to do'!? Must be Grace's influence but it does feel a bit funny. I'm not saying I'm usually horrible, except obvs to Luke and sometimes Mum, but that's only because they completely deserve it. It's just that I don't usually worry about 'being nice' and it sort of feels a bit weird to be thinking about it.

I'm not a mean girl and I'm not a bully. Definitely

not that, unless, I suppose, you count being mean to teachers, but that's not bullying — that's just being funny. Anyway, a kid can't bully a teacher. Bullies are people who are horrible on purpose to people who they think are weaker than them. I NEVER do that. I just like making people in my class laugh and being cheeky and giving a lot of backchat. I never said I was going to be nice to teachers. AS IF. Okay, but just in case, I won't tell anyone my brilliant new nickname for Aly in case she's all right. But if she's not then she's going to be called Dark Aly fo' sho.

AUTUMN TERM WEEK 1

TUESDAY (LATER)

I'm really cross. I've shut my door and locked it so no one can get in. There's only one key and I have it, so there. (When I'm not in I hide it inside Muzzy. Doesn't hurt her. She's only a toy, so, you know . . .) I am so CROSS. Grrr. I hate feeling angry. It makes me feel all jumbled up inside, especially when I've got no one to talk to. I can't ring any of my mates because I've run out of credit, and anyway Mum goes completely mad if she notices I've had long chats on my phone, which she can see from the bill, worst luck, and then she goes on and on for absolutely years about everyone calling each other on their mobiles, even when they've seen each other at school all day blah, blah, blah. Complaining about the usual stuff that no grown-up in the world understands.

MUZZY

Okay, so why I'm cross is because at supper I super caj happened to mention that there was a new girl, Dark Aly, in our class and immediately, without waiting to hear what I was going to say or knowing practically anything else about her, Mum chimed in, in that really aggravating sing-song 'I'm-only-teasing-darling' voice that makes me want to scream, 'Ooh, she sounds like trouble. She'll probably give you a run for your money in the naughty stakes,' and then Luke snorted and piped up, 'Huh, and you won't like that.' I could have killed them both. What do they know?! They've never even met her and I hadn't even told them practically one thing about her at all. They've, like, so jumped to conclusions without knowing one single actual fact. They are so annoying and know-it-all.

I might have told them what she'd said to Miss about her 'look'. She only said: 'It's a personal statement and I object to your questioning it.' Okay, it's quite a full-on thing to say but I've actually said and done things loads more cheeky and out-there than that. Mum and Luke are making out like they can already tell Dark Aly is majorly bad and so will definitely get into more trouble than I do at school.

I know this sounds a bit silly and like I'm jealous of her, but I am not. Well, I don't think I am. It's just that – oh god, I don't know, I can only say this in here, to you, if you know what I mean – I'm so happy now at HAC with my mates and feel really settled in, and I know that's mainly because I've made a reputation for myself with all the pranks and jokes and cheekiness and stuff. And it feels like if I stop being special and different because someone else, like Dark Aly, is more special and different than me, then maybe no one will be interested in being my mate any more. I don't know but I feel like I've got to keep doing all that stuff to stay popular. I like being popular. Of course I do.

But now I'm worried that she'll take over from

me and everyone will forget me and I won't be anyone special. I just want to be the naughtiest and cheekiest. You know, like The One in my year that everyone knows will say and do the funniest, most daring things. This probably sounds a bit pathetic and sad, but I'm not going to tell anyone any of this. I am going to make sure Dark Aly does not out-do me . . . Although I'm not really sure how I'm going to do that because, like I said, she is SO rude. I mean, she's, like, extra, and I really don't want to be like that. I try to be funny by deliberately misunderstanding things teachers say and making up things to be witty, but she's just downright horrible, and anyone can be like that. It doesn't take any effort.

Gran's just knocked on the door to tell me there's pudding, so I should come down. She's so great the way she knows how to get me back downstairs when I've had a strop. Mum would never come and get me, least of all for pudding. AS IF. In fact, Mum would make sure all the pudding was finished or hidden away before I came back down to make sure I didn't eat any. Hah, I know what I'm going to do. I'll make

sure I have a huge portion of pudding – that will so
annoy Mum! And, best of all, Gran will let me. Yay.
I feel much better now.

AUTUMN TERM
WEEK 1

THURSDAY

We've been back at school for nearly a whole week and I haven't been sent out of class once! This is not a good thing. I'm not saying this is a big achievement and something to be proud of. I am saying the opposite, in fact. And I must do something about this awful situation immediately. I haven't managed to do or say *anything* during a lesson to make anybody laugh or, almost as important, make any teachers cross, which is usually the same thing – me winding teachers up equals them getting angry equals everyone laughing. Erm, like, durr, and that's why I do it! I have been a bit cheeky here and there, but it's almost

like the teachers are used to me or something or . . .
and this would be the worst, because of Dark Aly
they now have bigger fish to fry. Aaargh!

Walking into school this morning I decided it was
high time . . . Wait a minute, 'high time'?! I've never
said that before in my life – high time?! High time?!
I don't even know what it means. It's that the sort of
thing that Granny Baird – Dad's mum, aka GB – says:
'It's high time you were taught some manners.' It
sounds sooooo posh! 'S'okay to use in writing, like
here, but I must make sure I NEVER accidentally
say it out loud. Honestly, the shame, can you picture
it? 'Hey, Emz, it's high time we went round yours!'
Oh man, I'd die of embarrassment. Anyways, I decided
it was time (i.e. not high time!) I thought up something
super cheeky to do ASAP. I can't have the staff
thinking I've changed over the summer holidays! No
way. Just because I liked that book I read over the
break (which I haven't told anyone about yet, not even

Grace) it does not mean I've become a goody two shoes!

BTW I'm not saying everyone who reads books is a nerd . . . Well, obvs Luke is an *actual* nerd but that's not just because he reads all the time. He's a nerd for loads of other reasons. Having his nose stuck inside a book all day every day is just part of his total nerdosity. I mean, A'isha reads loads and she's not a bit nerdy at all. In fact, A'isha is like the opposite of nerdy, thank god. And Grace reads even more than Luke, which doesn't seem possible but I think is actually true. She reads, like, a whole book a week practically, and although she is officially a nerd, I guess (she'd definitely say that about herself), she's not actually *nerdy*, if that makes sense. I think you can be a nerd without being nerdy. Yeah, I'm sure you can. Man, a whole book a week? I've just realised that's, like, fifty-two books a year . . . That is sooooo extra. She'll probably have run out of books to read before she's even grown up. There can't be that many books in the world!

Anyway, by the time I'd got to school I'd come up with three Guaranteed To Annoy Teachers Being Naughty options:

Option 1. Pretend I've lost my voice — that is sooooo hilarious. I do it sometimes to Luke and it drives him bonkers. It means I get to do lots of mouthing and miming and loads of I-don't-understand faces. And usually, this is the best, it also means the other person ends up whispering at you, even though they haven't lost their voice. Everyone does it — it's so random!

Option 2. Use some of the really, really unusual words I looked up in the dictionary over the summer with Luke when we were bored. We'd take it in turns to let the dictionary fall open at whatever page and then close our eyes and stick a finger on a word and then learn it. I've saved them all up to use when talking to teachers — I just know they won't know what most of them mean. Luke and I deliberately memorised as many weird ones as we could. Being him, he now obviously uses them for real when he's at school, making them even more convinced that he's a genius. I am only going to use them to trick teachers — much funnier than using them for real, obvs.

(My fave is PUSILLANIMOUS — absolutely nobody knows what that means and best of all it doesn't having anything to do with yucky pus, like you'd think it would. I've got loads like that — words that, if you have to guess what they mean, sound like they're to do with something else but then aren't. Oh man, that is going to wind my teachers up sooooo much.)

Option 3. Make sure my pencil 'accidentally' rolls off my desk about a million times during class — that'll drive most of the teachers absolutely bonkers — brilliant! And I'll obviously have to keep going under the desk to pick it up. Of course I will because they will have rolled 'ACCIDENTALLY' onto the floor. Fantastic!

So, first period, we had Ms Cameron, aka Number Ten (as in the prime minister, geddit?), and because it was her (she gets all het up soooo easily) I decided to go for one of my options straight away. I had been planning on not being naughty until the middle of the day but because she's always having a go at me I decided I might as well give her the 'benefit of my wheeze' as she likes to call me being cheeky! (If she catches me chatting in her class Ms Cameron always says to me 'Perhaps you'd like to give us all the benefit of your wisdom, Miss Baird?' in a super-sarky-I'm-so-hilarious voice.)

I decided to go with pretending I'd lost my voice. I'd just had time to tell A'isha and Emz (Grace isn't in that class) what I was going to do and I could see they were dying to see how Miss was going to react. I love that feeling. It's so exciting and makes me feel all jiggly – that feeling when I'm about to do something naughty or funny and I know my mates are waiting for it. It feels super daring too.

So Miss started handing out some sheets and told us we had to work on them in pairs. When she arrived at our table, I put my hand up and mouthed, but making sure no actual words came out, 'But there are three of us.' Miss looked at me like I was mad and immediately snapped, 'What?!' I caught Emz and A'isha trying not to snigger. So, again, saying the words with my mouth but making sure no actual sound came out, I mouthed, 'There are three of us, so we can't work in a pair.' A'isha actually snorted with laughter then. I think because I'd held up three fingers when I mouthed 'three of us', sort of like I was having to do sign language.

'I've no idea what you're playing at, Tabitha, and what's more I don't care! You can complete this sheet on your own. That'll teach you. Emma and A'isha can do theirs together!' Miss barked at me and then stomped off.

A few people round our table sort of sniggered but it wasn't over yet. I hadn't finished. No way. I wasn't about to let her have the last word and I definitely wasn't going to do the sheet on my own.

So I put my hand up and because I was pretending I couldn't speak obviously I had to flap my arm about to try to get her attention. I could see some of the class looking up and just knowing I was about to do something else, which was just what I wanted. But at the same moment Miss noticed me she also arrived at Dark Aly's table, who was sitting alone. So, distracted in that moment from having a go at me, Miss looked around, pointed at someone else sitting on their own, obviously to pair them up with Dark Aly.

And then suddenly, before she could move the other pupil, out of nowhere Dark Aly says really slowly and in a really spooky voice, 'Do not move that student to my table. I will not work with anyone else. I demand the right to complete this work alone.'

The whole class went silent. Everyone was staring at her, totes speechless, including Miss. It was so weird and random. First of all, what kind of crazy person actually wants to do any work alone if they don't have to? Second of all, she can't actually refuse to work with someone else – it's not her decision. Third, what was with that voice?! No one said a word.

I stopped waving and lowered my hand. It was pretty obvious I wasn't going to get anywhere with my winding-up-Miss-project if Dark Aly was going to go all Darth Vader (that is exactly what her voice sounded like!). Eventually, after what seemed like years of Miss staring at Dark Aly with her mouth open

— FYI, not a good look, Ms Cameron — and Dark Aly staring back at her without blinking once, Miss said, 'Very well, you can do it on your own.'

Can you believe that? This is the same teacher who made me sit alone at the front of the class the very first time she met me, before I'd ever done a single thing. And now this same teacher was not saying anything to a new girl who had been super rude — in fact, more than rude, like extra rude. She was letting her get away with it, just like that!

Dark Aly didn't reply, she just nodded as if she was saying, 'I knew all along you'd give in,' then she picked up a pen and started doing the sheet. We all looked at each other completely and totally amazed — none of us could believe Miss hadn't wobbled out. It was so weird and freaky.

I admit Dark Aly is pretty scary but, come on, she's still only a thirteen-year-old schoolgirl. She isn't *actually* Darth Vader. Just because she's got a miniature dagger stud in her ear plus a skull one doesn't mean she is, in real life, an axe murderer or anything. The way Miss had backed down was like she was scared of her.

Huh. Well, I'm not scared of her anyway. I was really cross afterwards because, thanks to that I'm-so-scary-weird-voice-wannabe-goth, my plan had completely backfired and I didn't get into trouble at all so I didn't manage to make the whole class laugh.

I hate Dark Aly. She can't be that badass all the time – she's going to ruin all my jokes and pranks if she keeps doing things like that. Oh god, I wonder if she did that on purpose because she'd seen me pretending I'd lost my voice and then waving my arm to get Miss's attention?! What if Dark Aly has decided to compete with me to be the coolest, naughtiest girl in the class?

What if she wins? What if no one likes me any more because of her? What will I do if I'm not the coolest, naughtiest girl at school? Who will I be instead? Errr, I don't like this feeling.

AUTUMN TERM
WEEK 2

FRIDAY

Oh man, what is wrong with adults? Huh, more like, what is NOT wrong with adults?! I mean, do they literally not have a single clue about anything at all? Sometimes – actually more like most of the time – I cannot believe the decisions they, supposedly as grown-ups, make! I mean, just take something huge like war or something not even that huge like what time it's okay to show programmes with people swearing and shouting at each on other TV – all those decisions are made by grown-ups, people who are supposed to know everything and have weighed everything up, but then when you see the decisions they did end up making you just think, Erm, are you a complete moron?

That is so true with what's just happened to me. You are so not going to believe this, because it is actually totally and completely unbelievable. Right, so you know Mum's ridiculous blog where she complains all day every day about how awful her life is, how dreadful and badly behaved I am, how hard it is for her to cope now that we've got no money and how useless Dad was?

Yes, that blog (and by the way, it's the same blog where she hardly ever complains about Luke. Actually, in fact, it's the exact opposite – it's usually stuff about how he's got an A in this or some teacher has written home to say how brilliant he was at something . . . You know, fascinating stuff – not). Anyway, it's the blog Mum's been writing since she split up with Dad and we moved to London, and, as if that weren't bad and super embarrassing enough, it is always stuff about how extra hard her life is as a single mum. (Does she really count as a single mum anyway if we're living with Gran? Hmm, don't think so. So, in a way, Mum is actually sort of lying on the blog too, as well as being boring and moany.)

So, because Mum was a journalist before she had me, and because as she keeps saying, thinking it's hilarious (it is so not), that she's 'parked her brain' (she means 'gave up work to live in the country and bring up kids', although I do not see what that's got to do with parking), she still has some contacts in newspapers and magazines, and anyways – oh man, I can hardly bear to write this down – some idiot has decided to make Mum's blog a weekly column in a newspaper! An actual newspaper that people buy and read every day, you know?! I might as well run away forever right now.

Mum is, of course, delighted, which, okay, is quite nice for her, I admit, and, all right, I suppose it is good that she's earning a bit of money, although they're not paying her that much she says, but, I mean, just how embarrassing is it going to be for me if anyone ever guesses that column is written by My

Own Mum?! Can you imagine the shame? If anyone finds out I would literally never ever be able to go to school again. Never mind school, I don't think I'd ever leave the house again, not even to walk Basil. Thank god the column, like her blog, is going to be anonymous so it's not like it will actually have printed at the top every week 'written by Katherine Baird, Tabitha Baird's mother'. Obvs if it did I would just die on the spot.

When Mum told me, she was so thrilled it was quite sweet, and I was happy for her. Well, you know, a bit. I congratulated her and stuff and then said, 'You have to swear on my and Luke's lives that you will never ever write about me,' which, you know, I think is fair enough. It is my life, after all, not hers.

And then, get this, Mum said, 'I am going to write about anything and everything that affects me and you'll just have to live with it.' Can you believe it?! It's like she thinks what I do has got something to do with her. It's my life, not hers. We ended up having a bit of a row and I really didn't want that. I wasn't looking for a row. I wasn't deliberately trying to wind her up. I know I sometimes do that but this time I really wasn't.

Mum accused me of being selfish and only thinking about myself and I said, 'Right back at you', because I thought exactly the same about her, which is actually right, isn't it? I mean, if she writes about me in the column, like specific stuff I've actually done, then it's going to be really easy to guess it's me, even if you don't know the writer's name. And then if she writes stuff about Luke or Gran it's going to be even easier to guess, isn't it? She'd better never mention Basil and his knitted outfits because there literally cannot be one other family in the world like us if you include our Westie and what Gran makes him wear. In the end Mum stomped off. God, she's so immature sometimes, especially when she doesn't win an argument.

Gran and Basil had been sitting on the other side of the kitchen during the row and after Mum left Gran said, using her voice for Basil, 'I think it's a big deal for your mum to get this job and maybe you should have made more of that before thinking about how it would affect you.'

I didn't like that. It made me feel bad and it was unfair too. I gave Gran a cross stare, but she didn't even look round at me and just kept clacking away with her knitting needles, pretending she hadn't said a word and it really had been Basil who'd spoken.

'Thanks very much for the advice, Basil,' I replied super sarkily, looking right at him and giving him a smarmy smile.

Basil looked back at me with his head tilted to one side and his eyes wide open like I'd hurt his feelings! I felt awful, but it wasn't even my fault. I'm never horrible to Gran and I didn't really want to say that to Basil, but then, you know, Basil shouldn't have 'said' that to me!

'Well, let's talk about it on our walk,' Basil then said (obvs actually Gran again).

Even though Basil can't actually talk, 'walk' is one

word he definitely understands. (A fact – no dog can talk, no matter what Gran thinks about her dog *choosing* not to talk!) So Basil started skipping about and doing his 'Ooh, a walk, I'm so excited' jig.

I was a bit annoyed because it's not like I had actually offered to take him for a walk, so Gran had just dropped me in it, completely taking it for granted that I would. I know it is usually, mainly, pretty much always, me who walks Basil, but people shouldn't assume that I will just like that. I decided not to make a big fuss, though. Gran's usually on my side against Mum but she obviously wasn't this time. I guessed it would make no difference if I did object anyway because once Basil's heard the word 'walk' he does not let you forget it. He'd have kept doing that crazy jig until I took him out, however much I tried to ignore him.

Obviously Basil and I didn't talk about it during our walk. As if. There was no sign of Sam (aka Snap-Dog Boy, cos of us having matching Westies. I hardly saw him over the summer but I still think he's totes gorge. That Sam. Not that I'm obsessed or anything, BTW). It was a bit drizzly and so, with nothing to take my mind off it, in the end, I did think a bit about Mum's news, because of what Gran had said. You know, of course I think it's good for her and all that stuff but, you have to admit, it is really weird knowing your mum is going to write private stuff about you in a newspaper where millions of people might see it. I mean, if your mum is a . . . a . . . I don't know . . . works in a bank or runs a business, like Emz's mum does, or is a childminder, like A'isha's mum, then their jobs have LITERALLY NOTHING to do with what their kids are doing all day long. It's, like, completely separate.

It'd almost be better if Mum had no job at all. At least when it was just a blog it was only a few other complaining mums who read it. Now the whole world is going to. Okay, I suppose her writing stuff is a bit better than no job. Dad's got no job and that is so lame. GB, his mum, supports him, or I guess she must do because he's got no money. If people ask, from now on saying my mum's a journalist, which I can (without letting on where she writes, obvs), is def better than saying she doesn't have a job, like I have to with Dad. Honestly, he's hopeless. It's so embarrassing. Emz's dad's got a job, and A'isha's dad's got two jobs – he's a postman and a minicab driver! No one knows where Grace's dad is because she's got two mums but both of them have got jobs! Actually, from what Grace has told me, it doesn't seem like she ever had a dad – well, not in the way most of us have one, because her mums are lesbians so they bought the . . . you know – yuck! – the ONE THING that only a dad can . . . bleurgh! Having to go into a shop and buy . . . totes mankenstein! Anyway, I suppose Dad's drinking is his job. Hah, hah. Well, he does do it full-time!

Hmm, I'll bet super-nice people like Grace wouldn't make jokes about their dads' drinking, but then maybe even super-nice people would if they had a parent who was a big drinker. You're probably not supposed to make jokes about people being alcoholics, but I don't see why not, especially if they're your own dad. I don't see why I should feel sorry for him. He's a grown-up, or supposed to be. I didn't ask him to be an alky. It's his fault we're all living with Gran in a tiny house now and . . . Oh, I'm not going to do this. I'm not going to waste my time going on about what's wrong with Dad. Anyway, I haven't got long enough. Hah, hah. It'd take all year! I love being in London and I love my mates and I'm so glad we don't live in the country in the middle of nowhere any more. I just wish Dad weren't such a waste of space dad-wise. Do you know what I mean?

Anyhoo, all right, basically, okay, I admit it, it is mainly a good thing that Mum's got this job. I'm just saying that I'll have to be on high alert At All Times to make sure she doesn't write the exact details of things I do. That is out of order – officially, as Grace would say!

When Basil and I got back, both of us soaking wet, Mum was sitting at the kitchen table with her laptop, tapping away as per, so I said it was good about the column. Man, she looked so pleased, and all I said was, 'Well done getting that column. It is quite funny

. . . if you're not me.' It's so weird the way parents get over-the-top pleased when you just do the littlest things that hardly mean anything! Gran shot me a smile to show me, I think, that she was pleased that I'd been nice to Mum. That felt good, but, oh god, I'm hope I'm not turning into a goody two-shoes!

I'm about to go to sleep and I've been thinking – I wonder if Emz and A'isha ever feel like they're more grown-up than their parents. Grace can't, she and her mum are as grown-up as each other! They're like two old ladies living together. Hah! They talk about books they've both read and politics and stuff like that! I am not joking. It's hilarious. I cannot imagine me and my mum doing that – ever.

I've got Muzzy in with me tonight. It's not a big deal and it's not like anyone's going to know but, you know, we're just going to have a cuddle. I know I'm thirteen but that's still okay . . . isn't it?

MUZZY

AUTUMN TERM
WEEK 3

SATURDAY

OHMYGOD, OHMYGOD, OHMYGOD. I AM GOING TO BE SICK. AAAAAAARGH! HELP ME! I AM LITERALLY GOING TO DIE OF SHAME, EMBARRASSMENT AND ... AND ... AND, AAARGH, OH GOD, I DON'T KNOW ALL THE OTHER THINGS THAT MAKE YOU GO HOT AND RED IN THE FACE AND FEEL SWEATY AND PANICKY AND LIKE YOU'RE GOING TO CRY. MUSTN'T CRY, MUSTN'T CRY, MUSTN'T CRY. PLEASE DON'T LET ME CRY.

Right, okay, I've calmed down a bit now, so I can tell you what's just happened and why I'm in such a flappy state. Here goes. I walked Basil earlier and bumped into Sam. I saw him first. He was on the other side of the road, walking in the other direction and quite far away, but when he caught sight of me he started waving frantically. So much so, in fact, that I realised he must really want to talk to me.

First, I thought, obvs, oooh, fantastic. He's super keen all of a sudden. What a result. Here we go, I am about to be asked out on a date! Gulp. But I didn't want to look desperate, natch, and let him see that I was thrilled that he was so mad to talk to me, so I just stood there and deliberately didn't look at him once as he walked towards me.

Anyway, so he gets near and then he goes all sheepish and stammery, so obviously I think, Oh my god, I was right. He is going to ask me out. He's definitely going to ask me out cos he's sooooo nervous.

I mean, that's what you'd think, wouldn't you? A boy you've talked to loads and see all the time, practically every day, and who is never nervy with you, suddenly waves at you to make you stop and then is super nervous when he tries to talk to you. It all adds up, doesn't it? You would think he was nervous because he was going to ask you out. That is what you would think, wouldn't you? You don't need to be a big-head – it's just that that would be the most obvious conclusion. Durr. Behaving like that OBVIOUSLY means he's going to ask you out.

BUT IT TURNS OUT, IF YOU ARE ME, YOU'D BE COMPLETELY AND UTTERLY WRONG.

Asking me out is practically the opposite of what he was trying to say. What he eventually said – oh god, I want to die – was, 'Erm, I don't really know how to put this but, erm, Bonnie is, well, she's . . . Well, ah, you can probably tell,' he mumbled, looking down at her.

I didn't have a clue what he was on about. I wondered if it was 'she's not really a dog' or 'she wants to come and live with you' or 'I can't walk her any more because I've got a totes gorge girlfriend, so can you walk her now so I can stay at home and snog my new gf all day long?' That last one would have been the worst, except it wouldn't have because, as it turned out The Worst was what came next.

Realising I wasn't going to guess what Bonnie was, he went on. 'Erm, it's a bit embarrassing this, but she's, erm, pregnant . . .' And then he just stopped speaking!

I didn't know what to say. I stared at him and he stared back at me and this went on for so long it was like a who's-going-to-blink-first competition. Finally he sort of shrugged his shoulders and gave me a half-grin like now that he'd told me this news everything else was as plain as day. I had no idea what I supposed to do. I couldn't work out what on earth this had to do with me. Basil was so bored he'd actually lain down on the ground by this time.

Eventually Sam spoke again. 'And . . . Basil's the dad . . . obviously.'

Before thinking it through I blurted out (just like Mum says I always do), 'How can he be? I mean, how did that happen?'

What an idiot. Luckily Sam is not Luke, so he didn't seize the chance to treat me to a 'hilarious lecture' on how dogs make babies. All the same, Sam did smile and gave me an 'are you serious?' look.

'Yes, all right, thank you,' I said. 'I know how, erm, IT happened, obviously. I meant how . . . no . . . when did Basil . . . The thing is . . . erm . . . Basil and Bonnie haven't ever been alone, have they?'

I knew I wasn't making sense. I was all over the shop. I just so didn't want to be having this conversation, least of all with the boy I fancy. I mean, please, you'd think, hope and pray your conversations with a boy you like would not be about dogs and definitely not about dogs doing THAT, wouldn't you? I could not believe I was talking about THAT with Sam. It was so utterly, completely, hopelessly humiliating.

Sam started explaining. 'Remember a while back when Basil got off his lead and chased Bonnie up the street like she was a squirrel covered in meat paste?'

I fake-laughed, pretending like I was actually remembering how hilarious it was that day but OF COURSE I didn't really remember. AS IF. When Sam and I are together I don't remember anything either of our dogs do, ever. I don't remember a single moment from any of the times I've bumped into Sam except him: his gorgeous sparkly blue eyes and glossy hair. Blimey, a bus could have turned over, cars could have crashed, both our dogs could have burst into song, and I wouldn't have noticed. Not that I am obsessed with Sam. I am not. I just can't hear or see anything else when he's talking to me, all right?

'Oh sorry,' I eventually managed to say, though I was super relieved because it didn't sound like Sam was having a go at me.

'Oh no, you don't need to be sorry. It was my fault. It turns out I shouldn't have taken her out that day because she was . . . erm . . . you know . . . in . . . aah . . . on . . . on . . . err . . .' Sam tailed off.

We both knew where this was going and there was no way I was going to let him finish that sentence, so I jumped right in: 'Yeah, yup, got it. I get it. Fine, yeah.'

'Anyway, that'll be why Basil ran after her like he did and, well, the rest is history now!' Sam laughed. 'My mum went mad at me for taking her out when she was, erm, you know, and letting it happen, but she's all right since she's found out what Westie puppies sell for. Hah, hah!'

I sort of tried to do another fake-laugh again, but I didn't really think it was funny at all. All I could actually think about was about how I could get away from having the conversation that I did NOT want to be having, even if it was with Sam, my current crush.

And then we just sort of stood there. Neither of us seemed to know what to say. So thank god both our dogs starting yapping and straining at their leashes at the same time.

Sam said, 'Just thought I ought to let you know . . .' and then he ran off after his dog who, I noticed, was pulling him quite fast for someone with a big tummy.

As he left I realised that that was maybe the longest conversation, if you can call it that, that we'd ever had – and was it about how much we liked each other or what bands we liked or meeting up maybe?! No, it was about Gran's Basil getting Sam's Bonnie pregnant – how disgusting is that? YUCKARAMA, totes mankenstein, and so definitely *not* what I'd imagined our first long chat would be about.

When I've dreamed about chatting to Sam and maybe, maybe, maybe ending up deciding to do something together, something sort of date-y-but-not-too-in-your-face-date-y, I certainly never ever once dreamed that our ENTIRE CONVERSATION would be about dogs doing . . . Eurgh, you know what!

It's just so embarrassing and, oh I don't know, sort of bleurgh and way too intimate. Actually I'm not sure it would be all right to talk to anyone about that stuff. Well, not for me. I certainly don't want to have a conversation with anyone about Basil and . . . that. And it's a million times worse that the conversation was with Sam.

Of course I love Basil. He is funny and he's so brilliant about wearing all Gran's crazy outfits. He never gets cross, not even when it's a cape or a stupid floppy hat, but I do not want to think about Basil doing that, ever — whatever he's wearing.

Oh god, this probably means I'll have to walk Basil somewhere completely different now and never see Sam again. I mean, I can't. I can't look him in the eyes now that we've had a conversation for HOURS about THAT. This is a disaster. Why did Basil have to do that and totally ruin my life?! Basil should have thought of the consequences. Yes, all right, I know dogs probably don't think about consequences, otherwise they wouldn't be dogs, they'd be . . . I dunno. Luke is always saying 'actions have consequences', whatever that means (apart from 'Announcement – I am a Super Nerd').

Oh man, this is awful. And BTW I am NOT going to tell Gran either. For starters, she'll want all the details – YUCK, I am not going through them EVER again – and then Gran might get all funny about the puppies and all that. She's always saying dogs are part of the family. No. I am going to forget all of this just happened. I have to erase all that MANKENSTEIN stuff from my brain and the tragedy of how Basil's yucky going-ons ruined my life.

AUTUMN TERM WEEK 4

WEDNESDAY

I've come upstairs to my bedroom because there is a really weird, stinky man in our kitchen. I don't know what he's doing here. He's got a beard. And I do not mean a trendy kind of beard a hipster-with-tons-of-cool-tattoos-who-wears-a-miniature-hat has. I mean like an old man's beard. You know, like he's been growing it for years on purpose – in fact, for so long it's got white hairs in it! Yuck.

Luke whispered to me, 'He looks like one of the wizards in the background from a Harry Potter film. The ones who don't speak but just stand around so that the whole place looks really wizardy,' which did make me laugh, because that is exactly the sort of beard it is – long, straggly and generally mankenstein.

It is def not the kind of beard someone young and good-looking would have. He's ancient too – like maybe even fifty years old. When I came in from school he was right there, sitting in our kitchen all caj, having a cup of tea with Gran like nothing could be more normal and happens-every-day-ish.

As soon as I walked in he said, 'Ah, you must be the famous Tabitha,' and Gran laughed. What is all that about? Obvs I am The Famous Tabitha (I like that), but I don't think he meant it in the way I mean it, like famous-at-school-for-all-the-wrong-reasons (although they're the right reasons according to me and gang!). And then super annoyingly he didn't tell me his name, and neither did Gran, which is a bit random too. I hate it when grown-ups know who you are, but don't tell you who they are! I wonder who this guy is . . .

Oh yeah, BTW I am going to have to do something really bad to Luke. I've got to think something up that will drive him completely and totally mad. He has not only used my, all right the, loo in the bathroom next to my room AGAIN when I specifically and totally banned him from using it because of his moronic inability to aim his wee correctly into the toilet, spraying it everywhere in the world except actually into it, but he's also left me a Post-it note about the mirror over the sink! I cannot believe it! I am literally going to kill him.

He put two notes (the big ones) side by side. It was practically an essay it was so long.

'DEAR OLDER SISTER . . .' What a twit. He knows my name. '. . . THIS MIRROR IS IN A DISGRACEFUL STATE AND REQUIRES IMMEDIATE CLEANSING WITH, MAY I SUGGEST, A HOT CLOTH AND A CLEANING PRODUCT DESIGNED TO BE ABLE TO CUT THROUGH BOTH GREASE AND GRIME. I RECOMMEND CIF, THOUGH YOU MAY, OF COURSE, USE ANOTHER

PRODUCT WITH SIMILAR QUALITIES AS
LONG AS IT DOES THE JOB.'

I thought I was going to explode reading it. God, if he weren't such a totes nerdball and had even one friend (apart from Mum, and no one in the world, not even Luke, can count their own mother as an actual friend), he wouldn't have the time to write stupid things like this. It went on:

'I FEEL THIS TASK FALLS TO YOU
RATHER THAN ME SINCE YOUR RECENT
DECISION TO APPLY MAKE-UP DAILY
USING THIS MIRROR HAS RESULTED IN
ITS EXTREME DIRTINESS. IN
ANTICIPATION OF YOUR COOPERATION
AND THANKING YOU FOR YOUR
CONSIDERATION. YOURS FAITHFULLY,
MASTER LUKE BAIRD.'

That is exactly what it said word for word. I am not joking. Honestly and truthfully that annoying little squirty know-it-all gnat wrote all of that in his best handwriting and left it up for me. It is literally THE MOST ANNOYING THING ANYONE HAS EVER DONE IN THE HISTORY OF THE UNIVERSE. Straight away, I ripped the notes up into tiny little pieces. That felt great.

And then I had to think about what I could do that would really, really annoy him as much as he'd annoyed me, and then I had a brainwave – the most brilliant, ingenious, utterly mank-of-mankenstein brainwave. Luke is literally going to pass out with bonkersosity. Got to go down to now; Gran's calling up. I will deliver my killer blow to Luke during supper if I get the chance. Gotta make sure everyone's there for maximum mankosity impact.

So, you'll never guess what – Dumbledore Chops (that's what I'm going to call the guy with the beard because that is exactly what he looks like) stayed for supper, again acting like it was The Most Ordinary Thing in the World, and like he does it all the time!

We never have anyone to supper, not even our mates from school. Well, obvs Luke doesn't have any mates so that's why he doesn't have them to supper because they don't exist, but I haven't invited mine to stay to eat. Emz, A'isha and Grace have all been here together once, but we went straight to my room, where we stayed the whole time. Gran did come up with a plate of biscuits, knocked on the door, told me they were there then went away again – she is so perfect. Thank god Mum wasn't around. She'd def have tried to come into my room and chat with them. Oh man, I would have died, especially as Emz and A'isha know about Mum's blog. I feel sick just thinking about it. Anyway, no one's stayed for supper yet. I'm not sure I can really cope with that prospect. Never mind the horror of Mum trying to 'get down' with my mates, probably using phrases like that and saying 'chillax' and 'no sweat' – a whole supper would be torture!

I mean, can you imagine my cool, brilliant mates sitting at our table listening to Gran pretending Basil's her son and speaking for him (she'd probably let him sit up at the actual table!), Luke talking about the activity of unseen planets, frogs' lifespans or how some fish actually swim backwards, Mum swooning over his fascinating (not) subjects and then going on at me about not eating pudding and nagging me to read more?! Yeah, thinking about what my bonkers family might suddenly do or say in front of my mates, having them over is probably the worst idea ever, especially if I want to stay popular!

So anyway we started supper before Mum was home – don't know where she was – and when she came in Dumbledore Chops said, 'Oh my goodness, Kat, how you've grown,' like she was a little girl. Gran laughed and Mum looked a bit like she didn't know what was going on.

And then Gran said, 'Kat, darling, you remember Frank, don't you? We used to work together at the council.'

Mum smiled and said, 'Oh yes,' but I don't think she really did remember him.

'Well, it must be twenty years ago now,' Dumbledore Chops, aka Frank apparently, said to Mum as she joined us at the table. She just smiled and nodded.

Over the meal Dumbledore Chops was talking a lot. Gran seemed to think every single thing he said was, like, the most amazing thing she'd ever heard and Mum laughed a few times too. And he was asking Luke lots of random questions like he knew in advance Luke would know the answers. It was like he was doing it on purpose so that Luke had a chance to show off. Huh, like he needs a chance!

And then while they were chatting like new bezzies I saw the perfect way to get my revenge for the badly aimed wee. Dumbledore Chops said something to Luke about telescopes and I immediately knew this was my chance, so I jumped in with, 'Why don't you go up to your room and get yours down to show –' I nearly actually said Dumbledore Chops (!) – 'erm, Frank?'

The old wizard looked at me and smiled. 'Yes, I'd love to see it,' so Luke raced upstairs and then we all heard him scream. Brilliant! Exactly as I planned.

I knew he'd see it straight away! Result! Before anyone had a chance to run up and see why he was screaming Luke came thundering back down the stairs in a mad panic, exactly as I'd hoped he would, holding the plastic bottle of wee I'd left in his room and yelled at me: 'You are so disgusting, so revolting. How could you do this? You are horrible and I hate you!'

Mum gave me a filthy look and took the bottle off Luke and read out the Post-it note I'd left on it:

'DEAR LUKE, PLEASE FIND INSIDE THIS BOTTLE ALL THE WEE YOU HAVE NOT BEEN ABLE TO DIRECT INTO THE INSIDE OF THE TOILET, AS YOU ARE SUPPOSED TO, I.E. LIKE A NORMAL PERSON. I HAVE SCOOPED IT UP AND PUT IT INSIDE THIS BOTTLE. I THOUGHT YOU MIGHT WANT IT BACK BECAUSE YOU NEVER GET IT INTO THE TOILET. YOU'RE WELCOME, TABITHA BAIRD (MISS).'

Dumbledore Chops actually burst out laughing. 'My older sisters were just the same with me when I was a kid,' he said.

Mum scowled at him, which he didn't see, and then at me, but before she could say anything Luke shouted at me, 'You're going to pay for this, just you wait. I am going to do something much, much worse to you! This is the most disgusting thing anyone has ever done in the history of the universe!'

I didn't reply but instead gave him a sickly sweet smile. Then I leant forward and took the bottle off Mum, looked straight at my annoying little brother and said, 'Chill, it's not like it's that big a deal.' And then I took a huge swig from the bottle, did a lot of licking my lips and then said all super caj, 'It's not that bad, actually. It'd just be better where it belongs, inside the actual loo!' Then I wiped my mouth.

BOTTLE OF WEE

Oh man, it was absolutely, completely and totally hilarious. Everyone howled and cried out, even Dumbledore Chops.

'You've gone too far this time, Tabitha,' Mum cried out, practically choking with shock. 'That is absolutely disgusting. I cannot believe you'd go to these lengths just to get the better of your brother!'

Luke looked like he was going to faint and Dumbledore Chops was staring right at me, his eyes wide open, like I was completely mad. Which, of course, if I really *had* scooped up all of my little brother's urine and then drunk it, I would be, totes! Only Gran knew. She was giving me a look like she had an idea. I actually think she even had a little smile on her face.

I waited a couple of seconds while everyone was groaning and moaning, letting them all think it was for real, and then said, 'That was actually lemon squash but I think I've made my point.'

Gran burst out laughing and Luke did smile but only after making a very long *bleurgh* noise. Typical. But Mum would not let it drop and starting going on about boundaries and limits and a load of other stuff that I could not care less about. I wasn't even listening to her actually. I couldn't see what any of that had to do with playing a joke on Luke to pay him back for all his millions of 'wee crimes'.

Honestly, Mum loves Luke so much she probably even thinks his wee is fantastic! Anyway, then get this, Dumbledore Chops pipes up, 'I think perhaps you might want to give your mother a break, eh?' and gives me the sort of 'Hey, we're all mates here but that's enough' look, the kind of super-annoying look teachers, who go in for all that 'let's talk about it' kind of telling-off, give kids sometimes. I could not believe it. A complete stranger – well, to me anyway – comes into my house and tells me off!? That is soooo extra. I was so cross I nearly swore at him but I knew Gran would get upset, so I just gave him a really long stare, shrugged my shoulders slowly and replied, 'Whatevs.'

If you think about it 'whatevs' is just like the most brilliant word ever invented because no grown-up ever says it, but whenever kids use it, it always, always, always drives adults round the bend. Major result. Cos with 'whatevs' you're really saying 'I could not care less about what you're saying', but you're not actually being openly rude – you're just saying 'whatever'. Oh man, I love 'whatevs' and I'm going to use it forever.

Luke and I looked at each other and I knew we were thinking the same thing – who does he think he is? And then there was a bit of a silence after that. I didn't care. It wasn't my fault Dumbledore Chops had made it all eggy by sticking up for Mum, as if she needs someone to do that. I'm not a monster. She's not frightened of me or anything. It was just a prank. It's not like I actually drank Luke's wee or anything truly extra like that.

And, as if that wasn't bad enough, Mum gave Dumbledore Chops a really big smile and said, 'Thank you for coming to my defence.'

Defence?! DEFENCE?! Oh please, like I'm an axe murderer or something. Or she's a fairy princess and I'm a man-eating bear! Oh my god, why doesn't she just marry him if she thinks he's so amazing?!

And then Dumbledore Chops, obviously all puffed up by Mum thanking him, sticks his nose in it again and replies, 'Well, I aim to please . . .' And then, smiling at Luke, says straight to him, 'So, why don't you aim too, please?' Everyone except me, but including Luke, the traitor, immediately burst out laughing.

Gran and Mum thought this was just brilliantly hilarious. I do not know why. It was totes lame and not that funny at all. Mum smiled at him and said it was 'a great play on words'. It was completely crazy. Everyone was acting like he'd put out a fire or done something difficult. He'd only made a pathetic joke. He hadn't saved us all from a hungry lion! 'To' and 'too' sound exactly the same always, so unless you say them in a stupid special 'notice how different I'm making these words sound' way, like Dumbledore Chops did, it's not exactly a brilliant discovery. It's not like it's some major talent or something. God, everyone was acting like he'd told the best joke in the whole wide world ever. It was totes ridiculous. Actually they were all just embarrassing themselves behaving like that. I didn't even care really.

AUTUMN TERM
WEEK 4

WEDNESDAY (LATER)

(I'm going to write LATER when it's the same day but it's later on. I saw it in a book, which was really someone's diary made into a book. LATER is much cooler than putting the time or 'The Same Day' or something lame and obvious like that, isn't it?)

Right before I was about to go to sleep Luke knocked on my door (good that he now knocks, took him ages to learn to do that). 'Just wanted to say that was quite funny with the pretend wee in the bottle and everything.'

I didn't think that was why he'd come in really, so I just replied, 'No biggie.'

And then he said, 'Do you think that man likes Mum . . . you know, likes-likes her?'

Oh god, that was exactly what I'd been worrying about before he'd come in. I sort of blurted out everything I'd been thinking. 'Dunno, he's a bit old for all that sort of thing. He's so old he's practically dead. Anyway, Mum couldn't like him back.'

Luke just stood there and nodded. Like he didn't know what to think but that he wasn't convinced.

I felt confused. I didn't want to be thinking about all this again. I'd just got all those horrible yucky thoughts out of my head. 'Anyway, forget about it. Mum and Dad aren't even divorced . . . so, you know . . .'

And then neither of us said anything for a bit and then Luke said, 'Yeah, well, cool wee. Hah, hah. Night,' and then left. It was good he'd thought the wee prank was funny. If he'd freaked out for real then Mum would have completely lost it with me.

BOTTLE OF WEE

I've never said the word 'divorce' about Mum and Dad before tonight. I've thought it but never actually said it out loud. I mean, I'm not a moron. Obvs I've wondered if they were going to get divorced, but, you know, I've also sort of wondered sometimes if they'll get back together. They could, couldn't they? If Dad stopped drinking and got a job and stopped living with his mum and getting her to do everything for him they could get back together, couldn't they? Things like that do happen. Hmm, don't want to think about this. It's making me sad.

Whatever happens I do not want Dumbledore Chops hanging around all the time. That is for definite.

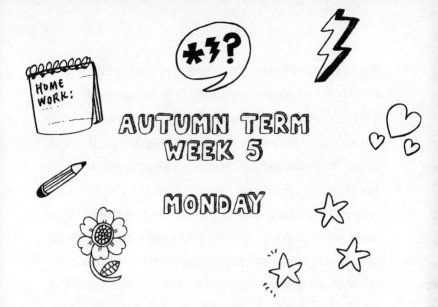

AUTUMN TERM
WEEK 5

MONDAY

Listen to this — we're going on a school trip to France for the day! How exciting is that!? The whole of Year Nine is going, Miss said. We're going the week before the October half-term. That's only three weeks away. I can't wait! Actually it wasn't a Miss, as in an actual teacher, it was that other Miss, the one who took me to A&E last term when I pretended to have had my finger amputated — her, the learning mentor, or as I called her back then an 'unofficial-police-officer-but-with-no-real-powers' and she'd laughed, which is how I knew she was all right. She is really nice, Ms Cantor, or Eva as she told me to call her. 'Just not when the head's around,' she'd whispered, smiling and giving us a wink.

Hah, that is so extra, isn't it? A member of staff actually telling you to do something but to keep it secret from the head teacher!? Random and cool or what, eh?

So, after school Emz, A'isha, Grace and I all decided we really needed to make lists of what we'd have to take to France. I know it's only a day trip but still. Obvs we're going to need loads of stuff, as well as the packed lunch Miss told us we'd need to bring. Me, Emz, A'isha and Grace were, like, all standing around outside school trying to decide where to go – no one had any money so we couldn't go to a café or anywhere cool to hang out.

♡FRIENDS♡

Can't wait until I'm older and I can afford to hang around all day in coffee bars tapping away on a laptop (I'm so totes always going to have the latest one, obvs), like practically all grown-ups do, apart from bus drivers. It's like all coffee shops are filled with adults with no jobs who are in there all day long. Weird. I wonder what they all did before there were so many coffee shops. Must remember to put a really snazzy laptop on the top of my Christmas wish list this year. Got to have one.

I was really worried one of my gang was going to suggest coming back to mine. I know I'm being a bit silly about that, because maybe, probably, we have been mates for long enough now for it not to matter how incredibly weird my family are, but I still can't help being worried. Would they go off me if they suddenly heard Gran doing Basil's voice, or saw Luke wearing that space creature's outfit HE MADE HIMSELF OF HIS OWN FREE WILL (he's always doing super-nerdy things like that), or Mum boasting about how her blog's become a column, or Dumbledore Chops popping round and trying to get 'down with the kids'? Oh god, see what I mean?

The dangers are sooooo endless. I know they've all been to my house before but they didn't actually witness any of the massive amount of horrors my bonkers family are capable of when they're full-on.

So it was a big relief when Grace suggested we all go to hers.

We all said yes immediately, even though hers is the furthest away, partly because Grace's mum always makes really nice biscuits – like every week. I have never seen a supermarket biscuit in that house. Grace's mum is such a Proper Mum, even though she's a lesbian, which obviously most mums aren't, I don't think. Still, what with the home-made biscuits and reading the same books as Grace, she is a totes Storybook-Proper-Mum.

So, for our lists, we decided we each had to take a disposable camera to take hilarious pics on the coach there and back, and a packed lunch and snacks, but more than usual so we could all share (this is very good for me because everyone else's food is always nicer than mine, even when Gran has sneaked in a treat for me without Mum seeing), a new notebook for making notes (durr) about France. (That last one wasn't my idea, obvs. Everyone laughed when I said that although I would take one I probably wouldn't be taking any notes and would just copy theirs later!) And then we couldn't think of any more vital things to take, apart from wet wipes, but, you know, there's bound to be much more we'll need. You can't have a day trip abroad without taking loads of stuff, can you?!

Grace's mum came in just as we were all about to leave and when Grace told her about France and everything she looked at A'isha and said, 'Oooh, you'd better make sure your teacher checks you can wear your hijab on the trip. France has banned all religious symbols and clothing. It's been a few years now. You'll probably be fine but I'd get them to check.'

We were all really surprised. That is so extra of the French, isn't it? I don't know how they think they can just say, 'You can't wear this and you can't wear that.' Random or what?

After we'd left and were walking back, before we all went our different ways, A'isha suddenly said, 'I couldn't care less about my hijab. I don't think it says anything about how religious I am or not, but I don't like the idea of someone saying I *can't* wear it if I actually want to.'

Emz nodded and said, 'Yeah, that's not really fair, is it?'

'And anyway,' I joined in, 'there are loads of girls in Year Nine who wear them and it's not like they can say every single one of them can't come into France.'

But when I said that A'isha stopped dead and turned to me with a really serious look on her face. 'There are eight of us max in the whole year who wear them, Tab, so not exactly loads out of what? about two hundred and ten kids.'

I could tell immediately that she was in a bit of a strop with me. A'isha continued, 'It might seem like loads to you but to me it's like there are actually loads of kids not wearing them!'

I didn't know what to say. I was so embarrassed and ashamed I'd said anything. I suddenly felt like I'd insulted A'isha. I really, really hadn't meant to. I was just trying to point out that if more than one or two girls wore them then whoever it is that is at the gate of France can't exactly point them all out and say, 'Oh, everybody wearing them isn't allowed to come in!'

I wanted to cry. But then sensible Emz who is, thank god, always the best at making things all right when things go weird, piped up: 'If you didn't grow up in a big city, like we did, A'isha, then you do probably notice things like that a bit more. We're used to them, but I'll bet no one wore them at your old school, Tab!'

I laughed, a bit too much, I quickly realised, to make everything seem all right. I was so relieved she'd smoothed things over.

But A'isha just said, 'Hmm,' and shrugged her shoulders in that way that we all know means 'whatevs'. Oh man, 'whatevs' isn't so great when one of your bezzies says it to you. And then when we all said goodbye, I could just tell A'isha was still in a mood with me. I didn't want to leave it like that but she just walked off like she didn't care.

WHATEVS

Oh god, I must make it up to her. I don't care what she wears. I don't care what anyone wears. I must make her realise that. I must, must, *must* make it up to her. I hate feeling like things are wobbly between us. It feels like it did when I first started at this school. A'isha was the first person to talk to me when I got to HAC and she was so friendly and nice. I'll never forget that. And now she's one of my absolute bezzies in the whole wide world and I've said something really stupid and upset her and I didn't even know I was doing it. I've got to find a way to make sure she knows I don't care about hijabs or anything like that.

During first period, Ms Cantor came in to give us some more deets about the France trip. (Eva, really, but we obvs didn't call her that in front of that class's teacher, Mr Proctor, aka Mr Proper. He is SO strict.) Just before she left Emz put her hand up and asked if it was true about France and hijabs.

And get this, Miss replied, 'Oh yes, I meant to tell you, I'm afraid they don't allow anyone in, pupils or teachers, if they are wearing any form of religious jewellery, headscarves, skull caps, etc. So that's no crosses, including earring studs,' (she was looking right at Dark Aly when she said that!) 'no Star of David, no hijabs, etc. etc. Sorry about that but blame the French. *C'est la vie!* Hah, hah!'

She said it like it was no big deal at all, like she was announcing we couldn't bring gloves or something. And probably for most people it maybe isn't that major a thing but at break it was obvious A'isha was really het up.

She said, 'My dad's going to go berserk and actually even I think it's way out of order, them telling me, or anyone, what we can and can't wear on a day visit!'

No one knew what to say and then I had a brilliant idea, and the best thing about it was that I realised that it was the perfect way of showing A'isha that I really, really don't mind about her headscarf or notice it much on anyone and that I was definitely her best pal.

'I've got a brilliant idea!' I practically shouted out. Grace, Emz and A'isha all turned to look at me. 'What about we all wear the hijab? Not just you, A'isha, us three too – me, Emz and Grace as well!?'

They were all looking at me like I was round the bend. 'We all wear them on the trip as an act of . . . of . . . erm . . .' I was wracking my brain but I could not remember the word. 'What's the word that means everyone does the same thing to show the world that they're all in it together?'

'Solidarity?' Grace said. (Of course she'd know the word.)

'Yes! That's it, solidarity! We ALL wear it to show that we're behind A'isha and anyone else who wears a hijab and that even though we don't wear them all the time we all disagree with the French ban,' I carried on.

I was talking a bit fast, I admit, but I was so excited. Everyone thought about it for a minute. At first I was worried they were all going to say it was a stupid idea. But then A'isha starting jumping about and said, 'And then that way it's not like a Muslim thing. It's like a statement thing. Like we're all saying we don't agree with their rules!'

'Like when there's a strike, everyone does it, not just the people who've been sacked or had their hours cut or whatever they're cross about,' Emz said, obviously thinking about it properly.

'Exactly!' Grace piped up. 'Like when the sixth-formers went on the teachers' strike. But it's the opposite of a strike, so instead of all refusing to do something, we're all doing it – we all wear the hijab!'

And then A'isha threw her arms round me and said, 'That is a brilliant idea, Tab. You are a genius!'

I wanted to cry I was so happy. I was so pleased and relieved I'd managed to think of something to make it all okay again with A'isha. And so pleased too that no one thought it was a ridiculous idea. I don't know if A'isha really had gone off me or anything major like that, but I was thrilled I'd come up with the idea . . . and anyway, it actually is a great idea. Now, we just have to work out how to make it happen . . .

♡FRIENDS♡

Later on I told Gran about it and she was really impressed. 'Tab, that is fantastic of you. How clever. That's feminism at work in everyday action, right there. I am so proud of you.'

I wasn't sure she was exactly right about that. I thought feminism was more about getting the same pay as men and answering back when stupid builders shout out rude things at you from scaffolding and all that, but still, it was nice that Gran was so pleased with me.

Of course, when he heard about it, pathetic Luke had something annoying to say. 'It might be an act of feminine solidarity but the whole headscarf ban thing is widely considered to be all about male domination and anti-Islam, so, you know –'

I cut him off right then and there, and told him to shut up and mind his own stupid business, which I decided was a perfect example of everyday female domination. Hah, hah!

AUTUMN TERM
WEEK 6

THURSDAY

Hmm, so not sure about this new girl, Alexandra. (Do you know what? I am sooooo right to call her Dark Aly. That is the perfect nickname for her.) I think I might actually have a major problem on my hands with her. I don't like it at all. I am really worried she's going to try to take over from me with the whole being-cheeky-to-teachers-and-making-everyone-laugh thing I've had going on. It'll be so unfair if she does. I've only been at HAC for, like, a term and a half. I've worked really, really, really hard at being naughty and funny. God, I nearly got myself excluded I was so out there with my cheekiness last term and thanks to all of that I am now actually popular for the first time in my life. Okay, not popular in a gorgeous-and-everyone-wants-to-look-like-me-or-be-me-or-be-my-mate way, not like in an American TV show, but, you know, in my way, a sort of everyone-now-knows-who-I-am-and-they-don't-hate-me-I-make-them-laugh way.

And that's definitely true with Emz, A'isha and Grace. I know it sounds a bit weird to be saying you're popular because teachers don't like you, but you know what I mean. I don't want to lose my reputation as The Naughtiest Girl in Year Nine. I want that respect. I earned it. Anyway, whatever happens, I am not going to give it up without a fight, that is for sure.

It's not as if Dark Aly is even funny. She's so not. She's just really moody and speaks in that low growly I'm-so-goth way all the time. So, thinking about it, if Dark Aly carries on like this and doesn't actually manage to make the class laugh then she's not really going to beat me, is she?

We had maths today with boring old Ms Drippy-Dry. God, she manages to make an already super-dull subject even more extra-especially-dull-with-extra-foam-on-top, as in DULLER.

How does she do it? I mean, who gets up in the morning one day and thinks, I know, I want to be a maths teacher? No one, that's who. I do not believe anyone in the whole entire world actually decides of their own free will to be a maths teacher. It's the same as deciding to be a dentist. No one's dream job is to be a dentist, is it? No one actually says when they're growing up, 'Ooh, I'd love to be a dentist OR a maths teacher,' do they? I reckon they're the jobs you end up with when you can't be whatever you really wanted to be.

Anyway, so we're doing this test that Ms Drippy-Dry's handed out. Though obvs I'm not really doing it. I'm whispering to the others about nothing much at all, just trying to put them off and make them laugh, because I'm going to copy Grace's answers when she's finished anyway, aren't I? Like, durr? Why would I bother to vex my brain doing the test when I've got Grace, who will defo get all the answers right, sitting right next to me. Erm, hello?! (BTW the only top set Grace isn't in is maths, which is just as well for me. Result! Though I don't know how that happened. Must ask her.)

So suddenly, from over the other side of class, Dark Aly says in that weird, really low, growly voice she always does, 'Are you having a laugh with this test, Miss?'

I look up – in fact, the whole class does – and Dark Aly's holding out the test paper, which admittedly is only one sheet, right at the edge so it flops down like a limp rag. And she's kind of flapping it a little bit like it stinks too.

'What, exactly do you mean, Alexandra?' Ms Drippy-Dry barks. Oh, she is not happy.

'I mean, Miss, did you give this out to us as a joke, you know, as in to be amusing?' Aly answers back, and then went on in a very spelling-it-out-for-morons way, 'That is what I mean.'

Oh my god. Even I thought that was a bit much and not even funny. It was just so horrible. At least I always try to be funny. Okay, that's probably not how the teachers see it, but the rest of the class do and that's what's important to me. But this, the way Aly was speaking to her, was, like, soooo snooty and mean.

'I don't wish to be spoken to like that, Alexandra Fletcher. Be quiet and just do the test!' Miss snipped back at her.

Dark Aly, who obviously wasn't about to back down, replied, 'I can't,' and then Miss barked, 'What do you mean "can't"?'

Dark Aly drawled, 'Can't, as in I. Can. Not.' Oh my god, it was so extra.

And then, weirdly, instead of blowing her top like she definitely would if I'd said that to her, Miss paused for a minute, stared at her like she was thinking of something and then just said, 'Right, well, suit yourself.' Can you believe it?!

It was like Miss was making an actual decision not to make her do the test, not to argue with her, for some secret reason that only she knew about.

Dark Aly shrugged her shoulders, slumped right down in her chair and screwed up the test sheet! She actually screwed the paper right up into a ball and flicked it across her table. No one could believe what they were seeing.

I reckon she must have wanted to get into an argument, that she'd wanted to really wind Miss up. I was sure she was disappointed when Miss gave in. I knew she was trying to get attention (takes one to know one!), but she was so grumpy and, I don't know, sort of horrible, and I think she also minded that no one seemed to be respecting the sass she'd given Miss. But we weren't because it was almost like she was too mean, if that makes sense?

I know I'm deliberately naughty on purpose and I know I do it to annoy the teachers, but the way I do it doesn't seem to make people hate me. I don't know how to explain the difference, except to say that the way Dark Aly was making trouble seemed more about her being angry than about having fun and making her classmates laugh. NOBODY was laughing, that is for sure. It was NOT funny. Actually it was a bit scary. Not that I am scared of her, obvs. AS IF. That'd be way extra. I'm not scared of anyone. Okay, maybe GB . . . a bit. But that's no biggie because everyone is scared of her!

On the way home (none of us really live the same way – it's actually quicker if we go our own separate ways, but pretty much every day we walk along the big main road so that we can hang out together for longer, which I so love) we were all talking about Dark Aly.

And Grace of course said, 'I think she's troubled. We don't know why she had to leave her old school. Maybe a horrible thing happened to her there?'

Everyone nodded like they were thinking that might be what was wrong with her.

'I know what happened to her there: *she* happened. She's the horrible thing that happened to her,' I said, and everyone laughed.

Anyway, even if Dark Aly's arrived, it looks like maybe I don't need to worry about her. She's definitely not making anyone laugh, so that's still going to be my job. Yay!

AUTUMN TERM WEEK 7

TUESDAY

Before I got up this morning, like really early, I heard Mum shouting her head off. It sounded like she was in the kitchen, downstairs, but I could hear her from my room upstairs. She was obviously having a major meltdown.

I got dressed really quickly (suppose that is the ONE good thing about being made to wear uniform, totes mankenstein as it completely is, at least you don't have to waste time deciding what to wear every day!), and went down. I wasn't that worried, you know, spesh because Mum freaks out about practically everything, so I reckoned it was probably that we'd run out of milk or something soooo not-major like that.

But it wasn't. It actually *was* truly major. You are not going to believe this. It is really hard to believe. Really hard. Mum was melting down because the post had come and she'd got a letter from our other granny, GB, saying that, wait for it, she thought I ought to go and live with her and Dad so that I could go back to my old school, Greyfriars, and – Mum read this bit out – 'benefit from a more structured life'!

Mum was spluttering with rage, then Gran took the letter off her and read it and then the moment she finished it she started spluttering with rage too. If Basil could read I'm pretty sure he'd have joined in with the whole spluttering-with-rage thing too. Do you know what was weird? Before I could get worried or angry about it, the very first feeling I had, and this is what was weird but really nice too, was how lovely and warm and cosy it felt having Mum and Gran go so mad about the idea of me living somewhere else, to see that they minded that much about me not living with them any more. I think I would have guessed that Gran wouldn't want it, but Mum is always so naggy, and so 'Don't do this, don't do that' or 'Don't eat those biscuits; you'll only get fatter'. (I absolutely hate it when she says that. She never ever says 'You'll get fat'. She always say 'fatter', as if I'm so obviously already fat, so she's really saying: 'Take that you are fat as obvious, but you mustn't get any fatter.' Do you know what I mean?)

I mean, I do know Mum loves me but I suppose until this letter came I didn't think she'd mind that much if I went to live with Dad, because then she wouldn't have to be always watching me, nagging me and controlling every single thing I do, which according to her blog is such a 'huge effort day in, day out'. (I am quoting from the blog, which I occasionally read, but don't tell Mum!) Yeah, and if I didn't live here any more she'd be free to go out with Dumbledore Chops all day long too.

DUMBLEDORE CHOPS
← NOT A COOL BEARD

Anyway, even though the whole letter was about me and what was best for me, according to GB, I was just standing there watching Gran and Mum stomp about waving their arms while laying out the breakfast stuff and going on and on: 'How dare she this and the arrogance that and the nerve this. She won't know what's hit her when she gets my reply,' and so on. You can imagine.

Basics, it was super clear that Gran and Mum were going to say: a) that GB could not have me, b) that GB had a real cheek even suggesting it, and c) a lot of quite rude things that they thought GB had coming (apparently!) and that it was 'high time' (hah, hah! Mum actually said that!) GB heard some home truths (whatever they are).

On the way to school I thought about it and actually, even though I've known GB all my life (we used to see more of her when we lived in the country than we did Gran because Gran lived in London and GB lived right near us), I still can't believe she'd think that I'd want to live with her or go back to Greyfriars Ladies' College. AS IF.

Actually that's not true. I can easily believe that bit

because GB can't imagine anyone not loving going to that place, but that's because she is posh and loves ponies more than people and lives in the country and all that. I wasn't like that 'country set', even when I was at Greyfriars and lived in the country. It is SO extra and typical of GB to be asking to have me and not Luke. You'd think she'd want him more, what with him being a super-nerd and embarrassingly brainy, but oh no, she wants me, 'the tricky one'. I'll bet it's so that she can 'take me in hand', which is what she is always saying. Really, though, if she was any sort of proper gran, like Gran is, then you'd think she'd want both of us. Especially because, according to her, Mum and Gran are obviously so totes useless at taking care of us. Plus, I do love Dad and all that, but I don't want to live with him again. I mean, how lame would that be? And I bet I'd go straight back to watching out for his drinking even though I so wouldn't want to. I just wouldn't be able to help myself.

One of the good things about Mum and Dad breaking up is that I don't have to worry about checking if he's had too much to drink any more. I spent so long before Mum and Dad broke up trying to pretend I didn't know he was drunk or that he'd hidden booze in a bush in the garden or in the dustbin or the bookshelves in the living room, which he did all the time. And I never even wanted to do that. It just sort of happened once I realised how hopeless he was.

It wasn't like I'd planned to be his guard. I didn't like it ever, not one bit. And I don't want to go back to all that. I'm not his mum. He's got one and he lives with her now, so she can follow him about all day long checking on him and his drinking. I'm not going to do that ever again. I'm not my dad's personal police officer. He is a grown man, even though you wouldn't think so most of the time! Plus, anyway, GB still refuses to believe Dad's even got a drink problem. Hilarious!

But still, I can't believe she was silly enough to think Mum would get that letter and just go, 'Oh yeah, fine, you have her. I'm useless at being her mum anyway, so here you go!' I think GB thinks because she's posh and has a big house that people will just do what she tells them to do. She is very bossy and,

I admit, a lot of people do what she tells them to, but they're only people who work for her or live in the village and are a bit frightened of her.

Mum's not even with Dad any more, so as if she's going to do what his mum tells her to do! Hah. Mum doesn't even do what her own mum tells her to do! Hey, actually neither do I, but then I'm not supposed to – I'm a teenager. Mum's so stroppy I don't think she'd do what GB told her to do even if it was 'best for me'.

Hmm, maybe that's not true. I don't really and truly, deep down, think Mum's a bad mum – apart from her excruciatingly embarrassing spilling-her-guts-about-every-single-boring-thing-in-her-life blog (now column) and liking Dumbledore Chops, she's okay. And I think if she really believed I'd be better off living at GB's and back at Greyfriars then she'd let me go, but THANK GOD that isn't true so Mum does not have to think about it.

But I am feeling a bit wobbly, right now, TBH. GB's not squishy and cuddly and warm like Gran is, and she never makes nice puddings. GB's all about long walks in the freezing cold being good for you and she'd never understand what I was feeling or even care about that sort of thing if I was upset or cross or stroppy, like Gran does. Oh god, I SO DON'T WANT TO GO THERE. I know I annoy Mum a lot, sometimes on purpose, I admit it, but I hope she won't let GB take me. She wouldn't, would she? No matter how cross I make Mum I don't think she'd be angry enough to let GB take me. And Gran wouldn't either, would she? I know we're all a bit squashed in Gran's tiny house but we're all right, aren't we? Lots of people live in smaller places. Gran and Mum won't decide there'd be more space without me, would they?

At break, I told my gang all about the letter. They could not believe GB had that kind of nerve.

A'isha said, 'Does she think she's the queen or something?!'

I replied with a completely straight face. 'Nah, she thinks she's much better than her,' and everyone laughed.

Grace, of course it would be her, said, 'To be fair,

she's only thinking about your education and if she believes that school to be the best then one can see her point of view.'

'One?' Emz turned to her and repeated it. 'One?!'

And then we all joined in and said it again, 'One?!'

Grace held her nerve, which I do secretly admire, I have to say, and replied, 'Yes. "One" is the correct impersonal pronoun to use in this context.'

'Yeah but it isn't "one", it's you!' I chipped in, laughing.

I wasn't taking the mick but obvs we couldn't let Grace use such a la-di-da word like that for the first time without saying something about it! I mean, I know she practically eats books she loves them soooooo much, but you still can't say 'one' in front of your mates and not expect them to give you a bit of a hard time.

Grace pursed her lips and looked at us all, giving us a sort of teacher-y I'm-annoyed-with-you-lot stare and then said, 'One is going to use any words one bloody well likes.'

And we all burst out laughing, including Grace. It was so funny, especially because Grace NEVER swears. Grace never really makes jokes, so when she does it is extra hilarious.

Must remember to try 'one' out on Luke. I've never heard him use it and he actually does sleep with a dictionary under his pillow – the stupid moron thinks the words will sort of seep into his brain that way. Durr. AS IF. He's going to die of envy when I ask him to pass 'one' the ketchup . . . Nah, that's no good. I'll have to think of something much more complicated than that. I don't think that even makes sense.

AUTUMN TERM
WEEK 7

THURSDAY

Something really, really properly bad has happened and I don't know what I'm going to do. I am actually, in real life, thinking of running away. I mean, I don't want to go to GB's, but I don't want to be here. I am so scared. I walked into the playground at break today and I saw Dark Aly with a group of girls, all from our year, around her – and they were all hysterically laughing. It was clear Dark Aly was acting something out – she was twisting her hair round one of her fingers and obviously doing some sort of imitation that was cracking everyone up.

I didn't care. Why would I? I've got nothing to do

with Dark Aly and as long as she doesn't get into more trouble than me and end up becoming cooler and more popular than me because of that I don't ever think about her. The only times I worry about her is when I think about that and even then I'm not actually that bothered. Okay, I am a bit but, you know . . . not majorly. I haven't even said anything to any of my gang, so that's how not bothered I am.

So, a bit later, Esme, one of the girls who'd been with Dark Aly walked past me and super caj I asked her what had been so funny earlier that had made them all crack up. I knew I was safe asking Esme. She's a bit of a drip so there was no way she was going to ask me why I was asking – like I would if it was the other way around!

'Oh, Aly was doing a brilliant imitation of those girls from that documentary series about that posh private school in the country. It was hilarious – she got their accent exactly right.'

I didn't know about the documentary series. How could I? We don't have a TV! Not having a TV is one of Mum's genius (NOT) ideas on how to get me to read more. She doesn't realise that I can watch pretty much anything I like on my computer online. Durr. Or that I am actually reading quite a bit these days anyway. (Just thought – maybe I should stop hiding my books from her and then she might let us have a TV.)

The way Esme said it, it was clear she thought everyone would know about this documentary but of course I didn't. I felt sick. I don't know why but somehow I just knew the school in it was going to turn out to be my old school – Greyfriars Ladies' College. I was sure it would be. Why wouldn't it be? Most of the girls there do have ridiculously posh accents. I never spoke like that, even when I was there. That was partly because I wasn't as posh as most of them, but also they were deliberately trying to sound like that and they mainly sounded like they couldn't get their mouths open very wide and like none of the words they used actually had consonants. Oh god, I wanted to die. What if it was my old school and anyone finds out I was there before? I literally do not know what I'll do.

Later on, back in class, Mr Proper (real name, Proctor) asked us some questions and really unusually Dark Aly put her hand up to answer. Everyone immediately looked at her because she never ever puts her hand up, so obvs Sir said she should give the answer, which she did correctly, but not in her normal Darth Vader voice, in the Greyfriars accent, the one Esme said she'd been doing in the playground!

The whole class burst out laughing immediately, even Sir, who said, 'I gather you've been watching *Through Thick and Thin*. Very good, Alexandra, most amusing. Now back to work, everyone.'

But he wasn't cross with her, like he would have been with me. It was so unfair. Even Emz, A'isha and Grace thought it was funny. I could have killed them.

Afterwards I was walking behind a couple of the really popular cool boys from my class (they are so popular I've never even spoken to them) and I heard one of them say, 'She really nailed that accent. Oh man, the girls at that place are all stuck-up morons,' and the other replied, 'Yeah, that'll be why the programme's called *Through Thick and Thin*,' and then they both did high fives and cackled loudly.

This is going to be the end of me. This is definitely going to be the reason I end up having to leave HAC. I thought it was maybe going to be Dark Aly, like if she got more popular than me and stuff, but this is way, way worse. Worse even than GB and the custody thing. What if anyone finds out that was the school I was at?! They'll all definitely think that's how I really talk and that I'm rich and stupid like all those girls there. Oh god, this is, like, the worst thing that has ever happened to me.

I've googled the show and it's actually called *Educating the Rich: Through Thick and Thin*, which I think is one of those on-purpose jokes, because it's true, most of the girls there, well, when I was there, are a bit thick and were all super skinny, which is another reason I never really fitted in because I'm so not super skinny and never have been.

I don't know the three main girls featured in the show. Apparently they're in Year Eleven – Venora, Gaia (is that really a real name?) and Plethora – so there's no way they'll be talking about me and how I had to leave because we were too poor to stay and because my dad was an alcoholic and all that horrible stuff.

I did know a Plethora when I was there, and she was okay, even though she was called Plethora, but it's not this one, thank god!

Actually it's such a ridiculous name it's hard to imagine finding a school where two girls are called Plethora, isn't it? You'd never find a Plethora at HAC! But still, what if some of the girls I was there with mention me in a 'We used to know this girl Tabitha who was so poor she had to leave' kind of a way? Oh god, it's going to be the end of everything!

I love it at HAC. No one here knows I used to be posh. And it's not as if I was ever even *that* posh, not posh like they were! I never had a pony, we never had a nanny or a house with a long crunchy pebbly drive! But if I am mentioned, anyone who sees it is obviously going to think that's what I am really underneath it all – not the cheeky, funny, fearless Tab Baird I am now. Oh man, what on earth am I going to do?!

This is one for Grace. Grace will know what to do. Emz and A'isha will probably just say 'don't worry' or 'chill' or 'how's anyone going to find out you were there?' Those three know I was obvs, because I told them ages ago before I ever knew someone was going to make a stupid documentary about the place and ruin my new life forever!!! But I'm pretty sure they won't take the mick and they def won't tell anyone else I was there . . . I don't think. They wouldn't, would they? Oh god, how can I know for def they won't?! Oh god, it's all going wrong. I just can't risk telling anyone, not even Grace. . . .

AUTUMN TERM
WEEK 7

SUNDAY

The new road where I've been taking Basil on his walks to avoid Sam was blocked off today, as there'd been an accident or something, so I ended up doing my old route, and even though he didn't see me cos he was too far away, I saw Sam and Bonnie, who is now absolutely huge. Those puppies must be coming any day now. Anyway, when I got home I made a very bad decision and told Gran about them. And Gran's reaction was NOT GOOD.

I caught Luke's eye when it all kicked off and although we were both trying really hard not to laugh I could tell he was as surprised as I was at how Gran reacted. OMG, I have never seen Gran go off on one like this. She is, in her own words, 'hopping mad'. Hilarious. I'm not saying 'hilarious' that Gran's upset, like upset-upset, obvs, but she did get crazy-angry about it all. Even Mum looked shocked, like she'd never seen Gran that het up.

Basics, what happened is that I, in a super-caj-not-realising-it-was-going-to-start-World-War-III way, let it slip at supper to everyone, including Dumbledore Chops, who was here AGAIN BTW, that Basil was going to be a dad soon and that the mum's owner was going to sell the puppies.

Gran literally dropped her fork onto her plate, making a really loud clatter and shouted with her mouth full, 'What?' A bit of spaghetti actually flew out of her mouth. Luke and I nearly choked to death laughing.

'Keep your hair on, Mum,' Mum said.

Dumbledore Chops, because he's always such a know-it-all, gave Gran a really long concerned look and said, 'Wasn't Basil neutered?'

'Of course he's not neutered, you idiot! If he'd been neutered he wouldn't be having any puppies, would he?'

Oh god, it was so brilliant. Luke and I both grinned at each other. Result. No one in our house had so far ever treated Dumbledore Chops like he was anything other than a Perfect Saint.

'Mum, Frank's only trying to help,' Mum chipped in, sticking up for him, even though he was Gran's friend first, which made Luke and me both look at each other and make identical something-stinks-here faces. I did not like this and obviously neither did Luke. It looks a lot like Mum might have 'special feelings' for Frank. Bleurgh, yuck and totes mankenstein.

'How far gone is the bitch?' Gran then asked, looking at me.

She sounded quite fierce. It was a bit scary because, like I said, Gran is never like this. All the same Luke and I both burst out laughing again. We just couldn't help ourselves. I'm sorry but Gran saying that word is super funny and I couldn't help cracking up. Obvs I know 'bitch' is what a girl dog is actually called, but you've got to admit hearing your own granny say that word out loud is pretty extra and super hilarious.

'I dunno,' I eventually managed to say. 'Sam told me a few weeks ago, so . . .'

'I am not having this!' Gran announced, picking up her fork again and practically stabbing her spaghetti to death. 'No grandchild of mine is going to be sold to a complete stranger, that is for sure. I am going to get custody of those puppies come hell or high water!'

Now it was Mum's turn to have a fit. 'Mum! They are not your grandchildren. They are dogs, not humans – DOGS! And anyway we can't have any more dogs here! It's bad enough with just –'

Luke and I immediately looked at each other, eyes wide open with fear. We both knew Mum was about to say Basil and if she did Gran would go totally berserk. But, thank god, just as she was about to say it Gran silenced Mum with an evil stare.

'Basil is your brother and I will no more tolerate you complaining about him than I would Tabitha complaining about Luke!'

Oh man, Gran knows it drives Mum completely bonkers when she pretends Basil is her brother, exactly as if he were human. Actually, Gran isn't pretending. She really does believe he is, but it is a bit much for her to pretend to her only *real* child that he's the same as her!

'For the last time, Mum, Basil is not my brother!! He is a dog who, by the way, cannot speak, no matter how much you pretend he can by speaking for him!' Mum was practically screaming by this time.

Luke and I could not stop laughing. We were getting hysterical and practically collapsing. It was absolutely hilarious. And even better, Dumbledore Chops looked a bit awks, like he didn't know what to do with himself.

I think Gran knew she'd gone a bit far because after a pause she looked at Mum and said very calmly and a bit sadly, 'How would you like it if someone tried to give away your children without you having a say in it?'

But Mum lost it completely then and shouted back, 'They are not Basil's children – they are puppies. Dogs not humans, dogs not humans, DOGS NOT HUMANS!'

No one said anything after that outburst, including Gran. And then she said very quietly and like she really, really meant it, 'Well, that's not how I see it.' And then, then, and this is the worst bit, Gran looked at me and asked, like it was the most normal thing in the world to be asking, 'Tabitha, next time you see the bitch's owner can you get their phone number for me, please? I am going to sort this out.'

Get Sam's phone number? Get Sam's phone number?!

Do you understand exactly what Gran is asking me to do?! Gran is asking me to ask the boy I like for his phone number! She is asking me, like it's the most super-easy thing in the world and a matter-of-fact chore, to ask a boy I like if I can have his number!!!!! Oh god. I wish I'd never said anything about the puppies! I cannot believe I've got myself into this mess. This is going to be the most embarrassing thing I've ever had to do in my whole entire life! I am going to die of shame. How is it going to go? What, like this, maybe?

'Oh, hi, Sam. No biggie, but can I have your phone number please?'

Oh yeah, that's going to be soooo natural and normal. Just a totes tra-la-la, la-di-da everyday question. You know, just like that.

AS IF.

However I say it and whatever I explain about the puppies and about Gran wanting them and all of that, which is the actual truth, he is still DEFINITELY going to think I've made it all up so that I can get his number. Of course he will. He's not going to believe that my gran actually thinks they are her grandchildren and that they have to live with her – I mean, who would?!

The trouble is, once I've got his phone number (I have to do it. I can't tell Gran I can't or won't. She'll be so upset if she doesn't at least try to get these blooming puppies!) I won't ever be able to call him or find out if he even likes me back, will I? I'd rather cut my tongue out than call him once I've asked for his number. It's so obvious and lame because he'll be expecting me to call, see? So obvs that I can't. Geddit? I'm just going to have to let Gran call his mum and let them sort it out and never ever call Sam for real myself. It's the only way I'll get over the shame of having to ask for his number.

I wish I'd never opened my big fat mouth. Aaaargh. Why did I say anything?! If only that road hadn't been closed then I'd never have seen Bonnie and never thought about her stupid puppies. It's all that closed road's fault!

I am dreading doing this. I feel sick. It is so totes THE most embarrassing thing I have ever had to do – Gran might as well have asked me to ask Sam to marry me!

Thank god at least I don't have to face this COMPLETE NIGHTMARE for a few days cos it's the trip to France tomorrow. So, major phew, I'm off the hook for a couple of days, but still, that TORTURE is going to have to happen before too long. Kill me now.

AUTUMN TERM
WEEK 8

MONDAY

Right, oh man, there is SO much to say. I'm still feeling all super jumbled up – sort of angry, sort of buzzy, sort of upset, sort of wish-I-hadn't-done-it, sort of proud, sort of I-don't-care but also, at the same time, sort of care-so-much-I-can't-bear-it . . . but mainly just got an extra-super-jumbly feeling inside my tummy.

We had to be at school really early to get the coach to take us to France – today was the day of THAT trip. Emz, A'isha, Grace and me had all agreed in advance that we were all definitely going to go through with the wearing-the-hijab-protest thing – the 'Statement

Headscarf' Grace had called it. We'd all decided we had to wear identical ones too, to make it look extra on-purpose-statement-y and that we were all in it together. Like it was definitely not a coincidence thing and that we all just happened to be wearing hijabs.

So, because it was all my idea in the first place, I'd said I'd make all the headscarves. Okay, actually, to be honest, that was Gran's idea. She'd suggested they all look the same and had offered to make them for us. For one awful butt-clenching moment I'd thought Gran meant she'd knit them! Can you imagine the cringe-factor of turning up with knitted headscarves? I'd rather have given up on the whole idea than have had to wear those! Luckily Gran hadn't meant that. Major phew. She'd got some old black material lying about and she'd run up a bunch of scarves on her sewing machine. Gran, as well as knitting, is brilliant at sewing practically anything, so, thank god, the scarves were just regular and normal triangles. Obvs, as we all know, Gran's knitted creations can be a bit . . . erm . . . random, as well as, let's face it, earth-shatteringly-life-endingly embarrassing but they're still pretty well done, even if they are a bit extra!

Even though we only needed four, one each, Gran actually gave me six. 'Just in case,' she said, handing them to me as I was leaving. Obvs I thanked her and everything but I didn't know what we might need an extra hijab 'just in case' for! It's not like they're knickers or socks or even sandwiches! Why would anyone in the world ever need a just-in-case hijab?

It was still so early by the time I got to school that it wasn't even completely light. I was really, really looking forward to the trip – seeing France and the whole journey, everything – but also really excited about doing our big thing. I suppose I was a bit more excited because it had been my idea too, you know. We were all going to do a Big Thing that everyone in our year was going to witness and it had all been my brainwave. Result.

My gang were all already there, crowded around the coach. As soon as I joined them I got out the bunch of headscarves in my bag. Everyone thanked me and said how brilliant Gran was.

'We need to thank our lucky stars your gran didn't knit them!' A'isha joked. So she'd obviously been worried that Gran might do that too.

We all laughed, including me, but although I laughed I did still feel a bit like she shouldn't have made a joke about my gran's knitting, cos, you know, only I can do that. Weird, isn't it, how you can make jokes all day long about your own mum, gran, brother, whoever, if they're your family, but when other people do it, it makes you cross? I wouldn't ever tell anyone else this but, for me, that even includes Luke, would you believe?! Random or what?

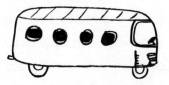

As we were getting on the coach, Grace and Emz, just like we'd planned, grabbed the first two rows of seats across the aisle from each other and then quickly bagsied the seats next to them. We hadn't actually planned that but it was just as well because there was no way I was sitting next to anyone else. Also, we needed to be all together and right at the front of the bus for when we did our 'mass hijab sit-in'. (I know it's not really a sit-in obvs, apart from the fact that we would be sitting down. Hah, hah!)

A'isha beckoned me to sit next to her. I was super pleased about that because I'd done all of this really for her. To make her realise that I hadn't ever thought she was different to the rest of us, or that anyone who wore something was any different to anyone else inside. I knew she still had the hump with me a bit, even though I'd organised the hijabs.

I so badly wanted this whole thing to work out so we could get completely back to normal. A'isha wasn't being like majorly horrible or anything. You couldn't put your finger on any one thing, but I just knew she wasn't yet totally okay with me. I really hated it being a bit different with her. It made everything feel a bit weird as well. I kept my fingers crossed that once we'd done our thing, everything could go back to normal. Oh man, but I could never, in a gazillion years, have guessed what was actually going to happen . . .

So the coach arrived at the Eurotunnel thing and went in. That was all a bit scary. Secretly I did not like the idea of going under the sea in a coach but I didn't tell anyone. I wasn't going to go all boo-hoo-crybaby-ish, especially not with what was coming, or so I thought!

Anyway, we got to France. Yay! Except not yay. All four of us looked at each other, nodded and then put on the headscarves. (A'isha put the one I gave her over the one she usually wears so that all of ours exactly matched.)

Miss (it was actually Eva, Ms Cantor), looked at us, made a face and then asked what we were doing. She wasn't super cross, she never is, but she was obviously a bit puzzled.

Emz and A'isha started giggling, while Grace just crossed her arms, and all three of my gang immediately looked at me, like it was my job to explain!

I hadn't planned on doing anything on my own

AND I hadn't thought we'd have to do any explaining until some French person asked us to take them off. But because it was completely obvious that none of the others were going to say anything I ended up having to explain what we were doing and why.

'I really respect this, Tabitha, and I think it's an important gesture but I'm afraid I can't jeopardise the whole trip for everyone to make a political point, valid as it might be,' Miss said, 'so can you please all take off the scarves so that we can get on with the trip?'

Now, I know I sort of actually like Miss and everything, but you can't decide to do something as major as this and then, as soon as a teacher says you can't, just back down, can you? But apparently YOU CAN if you're Emz, A'isha and Grace! As soon as Miss had finished speaking, and I mean like the actual second, all three of them sort of mumbled, 'All right, okay. Sorry, Miss,' and pulled their scarves off then and there, just like that. I could not believe it. I could not believe I'd gone to all that trouble and effort, and worrying about how to make it right with A'isha, and they'd all, including her, given in without a single moment of resistance.

It was like it had never been that big a deal to any of them at all. It was like they'd all forgotten how upset A'isha had got when she was first told she couldn't wear it! I was really, really cross. And I felt a bit betrayed. I know they weren't giving in on purpose to make me feel bad, but still – we had all decided to do it together.

So, without even knowing that was what I was going to do, I just looked at Miss and said, 'No, I'm sorry, I'm not taking it off. I am making a point!'

The other three all stared at me like I was mad but I wouldn't look back. I wasn't going to budge. Just because they'd all chickened out it didn't mean I was going to. In fact, weirdly, them all chickening out had made me even more determined to go through with it.

Miss gave me a long look without saying anything and eventually said, 'Suit yourself, Tabitha. We'll have to see what happens at customs.'

'Tab, come on. Don't be silly. Take it off,' Emz hissed at me.

Grace joined in. 'Yes, we've made our point. Take it off.'

A'isha didn't say anything. She didn't even look at me. I think she might have been feeling a bit bad cos she was the one who'd made all the fuss in the first place and now she'd taken her hijab off without saying boo! Anyway, I was not going to budge on this. A'isha was the one who'd made me feel upset by making out that I had 'noticed' who was wearing what and I was going to prove that this was not true – nothing was going to stop me.

The coach inched forward really slowly in a queue of coaches as soon as we got out of the Eurotunnel. At last we got to a barrier where there were loads of people in uniforms, sort of police, I guess, and one of them got on the coach.

Miss gave me a 'this is your last chance' look, but I crossed my arms and shook my head. I wasn't giving in without a fight.

I was going to go through with this. I knew it was crunch time. I felt really sick and nervous but excited too. I could not cave in now. Miss gave the French woman a piece of paper (with all the official school stuff about the visit on it, I guess). The woman sort of glanced at it, nodded and then turned round like she was about to get off the bus. I couldn't believe she hadn't noticed me in my forbidden-by-the-French headscarf. I was terrified I wasn't even going to get the chance to make my protest at all. But, just as she was nearly off, she turned her head and saw me. Result!

She got back on the bus, looking all serious now, and said to Miss, but pointing at me, 'Celui-là, non, non. C'est interdit en France.' I remembered enough of my French from Greyfriars (I do Spanish now at HAC, which I much prefer) to understand, but I didn't say anything. I just extra crossed my arms and stared straight ahead of me.

'Tabitha, okay, you've made your point, and the French have noted your protest, now can you please take it off?' Miss said. She, the French officer and now the coach driver were all staring at me like I was a major pain.

But I was not going to back down – EXTRA ESPECIALLY because A'isha, of all people, the only one of our gang who actually does wear a hijab, had taken off hers and she was the person I had started doing this whole thing for.

'I am not taking it off and you can't make me. It is a human right.'

I heard some of the class behind me let out 'ooooohs'. I was pleased about that. Luke (who else?) had told me about wearing it being a 'human right' thing. Of course I'd decided to ignore all the other stuff he'd said about depending on where you were in the world, blah, blah, blah. I just liked how official and serious 'a human right' sounded.

The French woman crossed her arms and stood in front of me while Miss sort of hovered beside her.

'Come on, Tab. Please take it off. We've only got a day here. Don't spoil it for everyone else,' she whispered at me, half leaning down, with her hands on her thighs and her head tilted to one side, like Basil does when he's trying to make you feel sorry for him.

I didn't know what to do. I did feel bad for her but I also felt that I shouldn't or couldn't give in. I didn't want to miss going into France and I definitely didn't want to make everyone else miss it. I didn't know what to do. And then, from a few seats back, I heard Dark Aly say in her I'm-so-goth-and-cool grunty way to whoever was sitting next to her, 'Just wait, she'll take it off. There's no way she's got the nerve to see this through.'

And although I am pretty sure I wouldn't have taken it off anyway, that did it. That was it. I was going to keep that headscarf on if it killed me. There was NO WAY I was going to prove Dark Aly right. There was NO WAY she was going to use this to prove that she was cooler than me.

So I put my absolute best 'nice' face on and said, 'I'm afraid it's a point of principle, Miss, so I'll be keeping it on.'

The French woman obviously understood and started babbling at Miss and waving her hands around and then she stormed off the bus, giving me a real stroppy look. Big deal. Who cares? She's not the boss of me.

Miss turned to me and said, 'Right, Tabitha, have it your own way, but you'll have to stay on the bus the whole day wearing that –' she pointed at the headscarf – 'while we have our day trip, or you can take it off right now and come with us.'

OMG, I nearly died! I hadn't thought about what would happen if I kept it on. I suppose I'd thought the French would just let me in, I guess. But it looked like Miss was actually going to leave me on the bus all day long. For one tiny minute I felt like bursting into tears. I had never thought that would happen. I'd never thought I'd be left on a stinky bus all day long while everyone, everyone including my bezzies, went swanning around France having a fab time without me.

It was soooooo unfair but I couldn't just cave in, could I? I couldn't go 'Oh all right then. It's no biggie'. How could I? Especially, extra especially, not after what Dark Aly had said. It was a biggie. This was huge. Not so much about telling the French they had stupid rules. It was about proving to A'isha that I wasn't some stuck-up posh girl from the country who thinks she's better than anyone who doesn't look like her (that's me, obvs).

Everyone was standing up to get off by now. I was the only one still sitting down. I could feel Dark Aly staring at me, glaring at me like she just knew I was going to give in at any moment. There was nothing for it: 'Sorry, Miss, I have to stick to my principles.' And that was it.

I literally sat on the stinky, boring, sweaty coach ALL DAY LONG wearing the headscarf because it wasn't like I could take it off after all that, was it? So that was just great. Not. And I am not lying. Everyone else went around France for the whole day while I sat on the coach! Apparently it's totes against the law to leave a pupil with a non-teacher i.e. the coach driver, so Miss got a bit flappy about that, which did make me feel extra-bad. In the end, though, they decided it'd be okay because he was the same driver they use for all the school trips so they've known him for years and he's been 'checked', whatever that means. It definitely doesn't mean he's been checked for not smoking, though – he stank of grotty fags! Even the driver went off for a bit to stand around with the other coach drivers. Not that I wanted to talk to him. AS IF. I was there for, like, nearly seven hours. Seven hours! It was SOOOOOOOOOOOOOOOO boring. And I ate the whole of my packed lunch really early, like at ten thirty, because I was so bored and of course I hadn't brought a book. Why would I? I didn't think I was going to be doing any reading, did I?! Luckily, though, I searched the coach and found a book someone had left on a seat at the back. So I read that. It was all right actually. But I did think I was going to die of boredom and starvation. However, no matter how mind-numbingly bored I got I just knew I'd done the right thing and that everyone was going to talk about it for AGES! So that made it all a bit better.

After what seemed like a million trillion years I spotted everyone finally coming back. I could feel them all looking at me as they got on the coach like they were just waiting to see if I was going to ask what it was like or tell them I'd been bored but I just smiled and said, 'Hi, hope it was fun.' And of course I was still wearing the hijab. Hah! There was absolutely no chance I was going to let one single person know I had been more bored than I had ever been in my whole life before!

!!!

A'isha sat next to me on the drive back and when we got into the tunnel and it was all dark she turned to me and said, 'I think what you did was so massive. I can't believe you did it. I'm so impressed. It's like the coolest thing ever. Anyway, the visit was a bit rubbish. I wish I'd stuck to my guns and stayed with you.'

I wanted to cry I was so pleased. It had all worked. I'd proved to A'isha (and everyone else, too, actually) that I believed in everyone and anyone's right to wear whatever they want to wear. Even if I had nearly exploded with boredom and very nearly died of hunger too. (I def didn't take enough sandwiches because, you know, I'd planned on sharing everyone else's, hadn't I?) I had made a Statement and that was BRILLIANT!!!!

Technically I can still say I've been to France, can't I? Just because I didn't – all right couldn't – get off the coach, I have still been to France, haven't I? When people are listing all the countries they've been to I can definitely say I've been to France, right? Because I have, even if I haven't put my actual feet on French ground it definitely counts, doesn't it?

I still think Mum and Gran are going to be proud

of me. Obvs Mum is going to go on about missing some boring museum or important sight, blah, blah, blah, because she's just like that. But I do think they'll both be impressed that I actually had the nerve to go through with the protest when NO ONE ELSE DID!

AUTUMN TERM
WEEK 8

TUESDAY

Okay, now that the French trip is over I'll have to take Basil out. This is it. I've got to do it. I can't keep putting it off.

I've paid Luke fifty pence twice now to do it for me on the condition he didn't tell anyone. But it's too expensive and I haven't got enough money to keep doing that and anyway he's bound to tell someone sooner or later, the little squirt. There's nothing for it.

Gran noticed I hadn't taken Basil out for a few days and reminded me that I needed to get 'that phone number'. Oh yeah, as if I'd forgotten that I have to humiliate myself – like forgetting that is ever going to happen. I could have kept using my brilliant other route but there was no way Gran was going to forget. I had to face the music, as Mum likes to say – why face the music, I don't know!

IF I see Sam and Bonnie (and I am praying to all gods and keeping every single thing crossed I don't), I know that I have got to ask for his phone number. I can't see a way out of it. I'm just going to ask really, really quickly in the most casual what's-the-big-deal way I can manage and then I'll run for it.

Nah, actually, thinking about it I'm going to look totes crazy if I do that and even more like I'm madly in love with him. Ridic. Running off is going to make me look like I'm three years old or something.

Okay, so I'll just really super caj mention Gran and in a no-big-deal style say she'd like to talk to his mum about the puppies because Basil's the dad. Yeah, I can probably manage that. Must remember to keep my cool, though: no sniggering and no babbling and def no giving him the whole story about Gran and Mum rowing about the puppies. Okay, here we go. Wish me luck. Laters.

AUTUMN TERM WEEK 8

TUESDAY (LATER)

OMG, you are so not going to believe what happened. It is soooo incredible and brilliant. I am so happy. I have literally just danced around my room. Did not make the mistake of dancing around in the hall again giving Luke a chance to say something sarky. I know it's a bit bonkers, but I don't care. I could burst I'm sooooooo happy.

So I did see Sam and Bonnie: they were way down the road from me and, okay, I admit I did think about turning back to avoid them. I felt so sick with nerves but then I realised I just had to do it.

So I kept walking towards them and when we met, like halfway, before I had a chance to say anything Sam said, 'Hey, my mum was wondering if when the puppies come you'd like to come over and see them, and bring your gran . . .' And then he smiled and continued, 'Because after all, she is Basil's mum, isn't she?'

I nearly burst with relief. I had to literally stop myself dive-bombing the pavement shouting 'thank you, thank you, thank you'. Obvs if I'd done that I'd have looked completely pathetic and desperate and that would have been way worse than having had to ask for his phone number in the first place, but you know what I mean. The relief of not having to ask HIM for his phone number was EPIC.

I couldn't believe he'd invited ME over, okay us, and at the same time saved me from the total shame of having to ask for his number. I know he didn't know he'd saved me from a fate worse than death but still it was soooooooooooo amazing that I hadn't had to ask. I wanted to do a jig of happiness. Yes, again, I know I would have looked like a total pranny, but I'm just saying that's how happy I was.

What actually happened in the end, and this is a hilarious turnaround, was HE said, 'So, give me your number and I'll text you when the puppies come, and then you can come over. That okay?'

I'll admit, I did say 'Yes, that'd be brilliant!' a bit too quickly and loudly and super keenly, but, you know, that's still MUCH better than having to ask him for his number.

Thinking about it now – it is sort of a date, isn't it? It does count as one, doesn't it? I know he didn't actually ask me out or anything specific like that, but he obviously doesn't mind me coming over, even if it was his mum's idea, because if he'd minded he'd have told her he didn't want me to come over and that she could forget about Gran seeing the puppies.

Oh man, I've just had a thought. What if it was HIS idea and not his mum's at all?! What if the whole 'why don't you come and see the puppies' thing is really just to get me over to his house?! That would be so amazing and romantic and adorable.

Erm, durr. Just thought about it some more. I am an idiot. Of course he didn't make it up to get me over – he asked me to bring Gran! Durr. Double-durr. Huh, more like triple-durr. What a dummy I am! No one asks someone to bring their granny with them if they're trying to be romantic! It must def have been his mum's idea. Anyway, never mind, that doesn't really matter. I'm still going to his house and he's got my number, so yay, yay, yay!

I must just make sure I don't get too excited and don't go thinking-about-it-all-the-time-y. You know, like, thinking about how it's going to be when we're there or whether he feels the same as I do or whether we'll be alone when we're at his or how many days it's going to be until he calls or whether we'll get married and have lots of kids and puppies of our own . . . STOP IT NOW! I am already doing it. MUST STOP IT IMMEDIATELY.

Okay. That's it. I am only going to check my phone ONCE AN HOUR, absolute max, every day until I hear from him. Hmm. Okay, that is a bit extra, isn't it? Cos that is like practically never. I might as well not have a mobile at all if I do that! Okay, so I will check it once every half hour . . . Hmm, all right, okay, maybe every fifteen minutes but def no more . . . except when it pings because then I can check it like I would ordinarily, durr. If it pings obvs I've got to check it immediately. That's standard. I'm just saying I must try not to check it more than every fifteen mins when there's no ping. You know, like you do sometimes in case a text or call has come in but you didn't hear it? Because that does happen quite a lot, especially when it's on silent like it has to be when we're in class. All right, so, okay, thinking about it, if it's on silent then I can check it as much as I like, can't I, because otherwise I won't actually know if he's sent a text unless I keep checking it. That makes sense, doesn't it?

AUTUMN TERM
WEEK 9

MONDAY

It is the end of the world as I know it. Official. I might as well give everything up right now. I might as well lie down on my bed, put my pillow over my head and stay there forever and ever. I am never leaving this house, ever. In fact, it's all so horrible, awful and mankenstein I might as well go and live with GB and Dad after all, because my life here is OVER. Mum has literally ruined my life. And on purpose.

You know Mum's stupid, moronic boo-hoo-poor-me blog that she now writes for a newspaper? A newspaper everyone in the world can buy or, even worse, read online? After she refused not to write the column, like I asked, I made her promise she'd never write about me in a way that would mean anyone at all, especially not anyone at school, would ever be able to work out that she was my mum and that it was me she was writing about. And she agreed. 'S'true she didn't actually swear on my and Luke's lives, like I begged, but she def agreed to be careful and only write about stuff all teenagers do. That is definitely what she said and she cannot deny it! But she lied! Of course, being Mum, she's saying she didn't lie and that I am being ridiculous and, get this, oversensitive. Incredible. Me being oversensitive?!

It's actually my fault, according to her! Right, and she's just being super sensitive and incredibly normal as per. NOT. Okay, so how many teenagers do you think have worn a hijab on a coach trip to France when they're not Muslims to start with?! That's right. No one. Exactly, none. Except for me, Tabitha Baird. I must be the only kid in the world who's done that. But Mum wrote about it in her column and, get this, she still thinks no one is going to know it's me! She obviously knew she shouldn't have done it. Because even though she won't admit it I know she feels guilty. I just knew she was doing something sneaky because she tried to stop me looking over her shoulder at her laptop and I wasn't actually even really trying to read anything. AS IF.

I don't want to read her stupid column. Why would I? It's going to be full of moaning about how awful I am and how hard her life is and what a genius Luke is. But earlier I walked past, behind her, and she slammed the lid down really quickly and then completely randomly asked me how I was doing. Mum never asks me how I'm doing. Well, not like that. She says 'What are you doing?' and always in that voice like she knows I'm doing something I shouldn't be. Or she asks 'Are you okay, sweetie?' in that voice like she thinks I'm a baby. Or sometimes she says 'What on earth do you think you're doing?' and that's usually when she's shouting. But she never ever asks 'How are you doing?' and extra definitely never in that sort of look-at-me-being-super-caj-nothing-bothers-me way.

So, that, plus suspiciously closing her laptop really

quickly, is what made guess she was up to something she knew I'd hate. I realised she was writing her column, but I knew she wouldn't let me read it, obvs. Anyway, she'd smell a rat straight away if I did ask to because I've always been so down on it. So, later on, when she was in the shower I sneaked down and read it. Mum's password is my and Luke's names – duh, like, genius. How do parents not know that that is every single parent's password?!

Okay, I admit that in the column she wasn't being horrible about my protest and the whole idea and everything. In fact, it read like she was actually a bit proud of me for seeing it through, but still EVERYONE WILL KNOW IT'S ME and that is a major life-ending catastrophe! I know everyone that matters to me already knows what happened and what I did – that's not it. It's that they will now know it is my mum's column, so if she writes about . . . I don't know . . . something super private or embarrassing, like . . . I dunno, something like . . . erm . . . say, me still having Muzzy in bed with me at night (which BTW I am actually NOT embarrassed about but don't exactly want talked about in a newspaper, thank you very much) or me trying to stop Luke using the same toilet as me (again, not ashamed of that but don't want the whole world knowing about it – even though I am completely in the right about that because of his disgusting wee) or . . . oh god, the worst, and I absolutely bet she will write about this: how I feel about who-Luke-and-I-think-is-probably-now-her-boyfriend – bleurgh, pukarama, mankenstein – Dumbledore Chops.

DUMBLEDORE CHOPS ← NOT A COOL BEARD

Oh yes. That is EXACTLY the sort of thing she's going to write about: how difficult it is for her because I'm, according to her, 'not nice to him', even though, according to her, he's so 'great with me' and understanding and calm blah, blah, blah. I'm the one who'll decide if he's 'great with me' and I've already decided he's not. Unless if by 'great with me' Mum means he's always here, always trying to 'get down with the kids' (which is what he hilariously calls talking to me and Luke in front of us but not to us – please kill me now) and always nodding his head the entire time anyone's talking in the most annoying look-at-me-I-am-listening-to-you-as-if-your-opinions-really-matter-to-me way, then, suuuuuuure, he is just GREAT with me. So, you see, once everyone's realised it's me thanks to the hijab story then they're obviously going to keep reading it so they can see what else she writes about me. Stands to reason, doesn't it?! I mean, I'd read a column in a grown-up's newspaper if I thought there was going to be stuff about someone from my school in it, who wouldn't?!

It is today that the column is in the paper. TODAY. I'm already late for school, but I just can't face it. I cannot face everyone. What if they've all read it and then they'll all know it's my mum?! Oh god, because of that, what if anyone looks up the old ones on her blog? There'll be worse-than-death ones. I am sure she'll have written about Dad and his drinking, them breaking up, Dad losing all the money we ever had, having to sell the house . . .

Ohgodohgodohgodohgodohgod. I've just thought – what if she's ever written about me having been at Greyfriars Ladies' College?! Then they are ALL going to know I was at the school in the documentary. They're going to think I was like all those girls, that I used to talk in the same ridiculous accent those girls do, and even though they'd be wrong they're going to think that all I ever wanted was an all-over tan and a pony!!!! Oh god, I don't know what to do. I can't go in if anyone at all has read it. I just can't.

My phone's just pinged. It's school saying I'll get a detention if I'm not there before second period. I already know that. Everyone knows that's what happens if you're late. Hah, a detention?! If anyone's seen the column and worked out it's written by my mum they might as well get ready to give me detention for the rest of my life because I am NEVER going back to school if they have. That is DEFINITE.

AUTUMN TERM
WEEK 9

MONDAY (LATER)

Huh. I don't know what to think. It's all a bit weird. I feel a bit funny. I am NOT used to this feeling. Today did NOT go how I expected, thank god. Got to school, right, and managed to slip in before period two started. My super pal A'isha told me she'd made an excuse for why I wasn't at registration (and they believed her, durr!) and then I thought I was going to die. It was ECS (education, culture and society, the longest and most boring way in the world of saying RE, which apparently you're not allowed to say any more) and just as class started I saw Miss (it was Ms Cantor aka Eva), had a copy of the newspaper Mum's column is in on her desk.

I went all hot and panicky. Just like I'd been scared of and the reason I'd been late. My absolute worst nightmare was coming true. It was going to happen. I was sure – even though I've always thought she was nice, the nicest teacher actually – I just knew she was going to read it out aloud to the whole class. And then it happened. It was all sort of in slow motion, like watching a horrible car crash or something. I wanted to run as fast as I could out of the class.

Miss stood up and opened the newspaper at *exactly* the place I knew Mum's column was. I knew this was the end of my life; I just knew it was all over. I stared at the floor wishing with all my might it would open up and swallow me up. I'd broken into a sweat. It was all I could do to stop myself bursting into tears.

'Class, I was going to talk to you about acts of kindness today and then I saw this in the paper and I thought it would be the perfect illustration of how a small act can carry a great deal of power,' Miss said to us all.

Of course I was the only one who knew what was coming. And then she started to read the column aloud. I was so upset and panic-stricken it took me a few minutes to realise that even though it was Mum's column it wasn't about the whole hijab thing. It was nearly that story but it was about a teenage girl who, even though she wasn't Jewish, had worn a Star of David necklace because one of her bezzies was Jewish and the school they were at wouldn't allow them to wear any jewellery, so she'd worn it out of 'solidarity'.

I wanted to jump for joy I was so relieved. I could not believe Mum had changed her story. I was sooooo pleased. I just wanted to dance around the room, going 'That's not me, that's not me. Everybody, that is not me!', but luckily I quickly realised that (apart from looking like a total loon) saying 'That's not me' would make most people immediately guess that it was of course me!

I was so grateful to Mum . . . not that I should be that grateful actually, you know, because she should never have written it in the first place, but still I was very, VERY pleased.

As soon as I got home I ran in and gave Mum a big hug. 'That's a lovely treat. What's it for?' Mum said, looking at me and pushing my hair away from my face, which I usually hate but this time it was okay . . . it was sort of nice. It was a bit like being little again.

'You know,' I replied.

She gave me a big smile and said, 'I was very proud of what you did, you know?' I hadn't actually known, so it was nice to hear. And then I went upstairs, because TBH I didn't want the whole thing to turn into a blub fest. Obvs I love Mum to bits and everything but I can't hang about all day letting her hug me. I am not a toddler!

Mum called up the stairs just as I got to my room. 'By the way, darling, it was Frank who persuaded me to change the column . . . not to put you and the hijab thing in it. So maybe he's not a complete monster . . .'

I didn't reply, though. I mean, so what? Who cares? Dumbledore Chops probably only did it so that Mum would tell me and I'll suddenly love him because of it. Big deal. Hmm, I am grateful, though . . . Obvs not to him. I didn't ask him to do anything . . . Still, it is a very good thing that she didn't put that stuff in . . . so, you know, I guess that was nice of him to talk to her . . . but I'm not going to thank him or anything extra like that. It was his decision, not mine. I didn't ask him to interfere, so, you know . . . that's on him.

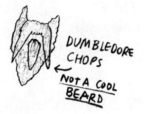

DUMBLEDORE CHOPS
← NOT A COOL BEARD

Oh yeah, meant to say, get this, after Miss had read the column out she asked us all what we thought. As you can probably guess I was super terrified someone might guess it was written by my mum. Obvs there was absolutely no reason to guess that. How could anyone? It's just because I thought someone might guess because of how panicky I had looked.

And then Dark Aly put her hand up and said,

'That's a bit like what Tab did with the hijab and the trip to France, isn't it?'

I thought I was going to be sick at first, because I was sure she knew it was my mum and was making sure everyone else realised that the story was actually about me and that she was taking the mick. Emz, A'isha and Grace all stared at me. I could tell they were all thinking what I was thinking: does she know it's sort of about you?

No one knew what to do. If Dark Aly had guessed the truth then I was done for. I nearly passed out with terror.

But then, before any of us had a chance to think up something to say that might put Dark Aly off the scent, she said, 'Yeah, that was pretty cool. There's no way any of those morons from that ladies' college in the documentary would do a thing like that.' And then she looked over and nodded at me – in exactly the same way the really cool boys nod at each other in the corridor when they don't know each other well enough to stop and talk. You know, how they nod to sort of say 'We're not going to stop and talk because we're not mates but . . . I know you who are . . . respect.'

I am sure that is what Dark Aly was saying to me with her nod and even though I don't actually think she is cooler than me I will admit that she is definitely scarier so it was pretty great that she'd said that – in fact, it was completely brilliant that she'd said that about the documentary. So she definitely doesn't know I went to there. And of course, nearly as brilliant, she obvs didn't know the column was written by my mum or was, in fact, anything to do with me at all. MAJOR PHEW plus MAJOR RESULT.

AAAAAAAAARGH - today is THE day! Oh man, I am soooo nervous. I'm super excited too but mainly nervous. Aaaaaaaargh.

Today is the day Gran and I go to Sam's. I AM GOING TO SAM'S HOUSE. Oh yes! He finally texted me after nearly a whole week. I must have checked my phone three thousand gazillion times a day since I gave him my number. And I kept my mobile on all night too and next to me in bed, which of course means I have been woken up, like, practically a billion times in the middle of the night every night this last week by stupid moronic robots asking me if they can help me collect my pension (pension, hello?! I'm thirteen!) or get some money for the accident I might not remember having. Like, durr, if you've had an accident I think you might just remember having it!

I was beginning to think Sam was never going to call, that maybe he'd regretted suggesting we come round or that he'd realised I liked him and didn't want me to come round if I liked him in 'that' way because he already knew he didn't like me back in THAT way. Actually after a couple of days of not getting any texts or anything from him and weirdly not seeing him now that I was using the old walking route again I started worrying that he'd maybe been in some horrible accident or died or worse – I didn't know what! And then I started really panicking in case he was deliberately taking Bonnie out for walks at different times precisely so that he wouldn't bump into me because he regretted asking us over. Anyway, I did get a text from him AT LAST inviting Gran and me (and Basil, which was super sweet of him) round to tea today, Saturday.

I am soooooooo glad he didn't suggest a school

day because then I'd have had no time to get dressed properly. I'd have just had to come straight in from school and change and rush out and not properly prepare what I was wearing and how I looked and everything. Okay, look, I know it's not An Actual Date and I'm not saying my whole life revolves around Sam and what he thinks of me but, you know, I don't want to turn up looking all I've-been-at-school-all-day-ish. Hmm, just thinking about that, must also make sure I don't turn up looking like I've thought and planned how to look for far too long either. That'd make me look like I'd come straight from the Desperate Department!

EAT ME

CHOCOLATE BISCUITS

We're invited for four p.m. Tea, the text said. I guess that means tea, as in the drink and biscuits, yeah? Must remember not eat too many biscuits. Hah – Mum would be pleased if she saw I'd written that! I don't care really how many biscuits I eat, but I don't want to look like a fat person who always eats tons of biscuits. Funny, isn't it, you always think someone looks fatter if see them eating fattening things, don't you? Even if they're not actually that fat at all. Or maybe that's just me. Maybe only I do that because of Mum always going on about 'Don't eat this, don't eat that'. Hmm. Yeah, thinking about it, it's Mum's fault I feel fat sometimes because I only ever feel fat when she tells me I shouldn't be eating something.

Anyway, so I'm going to wear my super-cool ripped-at-the-knee black jeans, my new and completely fantastic and gorge in every way pink DMs and my big baggy sweater because that will totes caj down the whole outfit, and make it look like I haven't thought about what to wear every single minute of every single day since I got the invitation, which of course I have, but I can't look like that's what I've done, obvs.

Also, I don't want to look like it's the first time I've ever been to a-boy-I-like's house. I know IT IS the first time I've done that – ever – but my outfit doesn't need to shout that out, does it? I mean, Mum (who doesn't even know I like Sam or anything about him, thank god) suggested I wear that red dress she bought me last Christmas!!!! Is she completely mad?! Wear a dress?! I like the dress, you know, but hello: a) it is a dress, which is about exactly the same as wearing something with PLEASE LOOK AT ME. I HAVE DRESSED UP SPECIALLY FOR YOU written across the front of it, b) it is red and red is also just about the most PLEASE LOOK AT ME colour ever invented, and c) who wears a dress to go and meet dogs?!

I know I've met Bonnie, Sam's mum's dog (can you say 'met' when you're talking about animals? I know Gran would!) but still, we're going to the house to 'meet' (?!) her and her family properly.

Oh god, I've just thought. Please, please, please, do not let Gran say anything about including Basil in the conversation or let her talk for him or say what he's 'thinking'. I will die of shame. I want to look super cool at Sam's and not like I'm directly related to a person who is completely bonkers! Gran is great and I love her to bits of course, but, you know, I don't want people I hardly know thinking 'Hellooooo?! A talking dog? Is she crazy?'

TBH I know deep down Gran doesn't really, really, *really* believe Basil can talk, but she believes for sure that he understands everything, and she most definitely believes he ACTUALLY LIKES all those knitted outfits she makes for him. Yeah, thinking about all that, I can see how that would make her sound like a Proper Bonkers Person to someone who doesn't know her like I do. How am I going to let Sam and his mum know that I don't believe all the stuff Gran believes about Basil if she does start talking about him as if he was human?! I want to be loyal to Gran, but I don't want anyone to think I'm like she is about her dog.

It's really hard sometimes to be on someone's side but also to let other people know you're kind of against them when they're a bit extra. It's a bit like that with Grace sometimes when she is so ridiculously super-swot-of-the-century, and like so extra with homework, knowledge, facts, etc. that you can just see others at school looking at her like 'Are you for real?' and then giving us other three looks like they're expecting us to agree with them. It's SO hard not to give them back looks like 'Yeah, we know! What is she like?!' And it's especially hard for me, because everyone knows I'm the one who never really does homework and all that, so they're def expecting me to give them that kind of look back or to say something kind of putting Grace down. But I can't and I don't really want to.

I want to be popular and cool but I do not want to be one of those people who have a gang of bezzies who they'll immediately be horrible about when they're not with them so that everyone thinks they're cool. But it is sooooo hard sometimes. Grace is just not cool. Fact.

Actually that's not true. She is cool because she is so totes happy to be her own kind of person and doesn't worry about what others think of her. She's just not like regular-cool, I guess, which I suppose kind of makes her super cool in the end, if you think about it. Anyway, I'm glad she's one of us now but

I'd still rather be my kind of cool than her kind of cool. Maybe there's room for all kinds of cool . . . There should be anyway really, shouldn't there?

Like Dark Aly, for example. I mean, she isn't that bad after all. Don't get me wrong, I'm not about to become her bezzy or anything like that, but she's not quite as grumpy and leave-me-alone-y and as in-your-face-goth as she makes out. In a way, I actually think she maybe sort of wants to be included a bit more . . . you know how sometimes when you need something you actually pretend you extra don't need it? Her so-super-cool-I'm-frosty might all be a front.

Sam *is* cool, that is for sure. Soooooo cool. Tall, with lush brown glossy hair and he's really funny. Sam is regular-cool, not quirky-cool like Grace, which I'm super pleased about. Can't wait to go over and hang out with him. Oh man, if he asks me out properly after this we might become a couple and then we could walk our dogs together at the same time and maybe be like a cool couple with matching dogs – and how cool is that?!

AUTUMN TERM
WEEK 9

SATURDAY (LATER)

Oh, I don't know how to begin. I am really cross. And I'm really angry. And I am upset too, obvs, but mainly angry and cross. I don't know if Gran's to blame or Sam's mum or what. No, actually I know Gran's not to blame. But I do know it's all gone wrong and horrid, and I hate Sam and his stuck-up mum. Sam is not cool. Sam is the complete opposite of cool. And I am never ever going to talk to him again as long as I live.

Gran and I went to Sam's house. It's huge! Well, much bigger than ours anyway. It's up that swanky road, which is fine, you know, but walking up to their front door, which you get to up steps at the end of a long garden path, did feel a bit scary. For a horrible minute I thought a butler might answer the front door but, thank god, it was Sam and Bonnie who started yapping away as soon as she saw Basil.

And then Sam's mum appeared. 'Hello, welcome. I'm Samantha, Sam's mum,' she said as she walked towards us. 'And this must be naughty, naughty Basil,' she continued, kneeling down and wagging her finger at Basil right in front of his face.

If I'd been him I'd have bitten it off. I thought it was a bit rude, greeting us like that. He's not naughty. He just did what all dogs do when girl dogs are around who are . . . bleurgh . . . you know. Anyway, I did think it was a bit extra of her to say that when she was meeting us for the very first time. It felt like she was saying 'You two obviously have to agree with me that this is all Basil's fault' straight away.

Gran just smiled and handed her the cake she'd made, one of her delish Victoria sponges. Samantha (who gives their kid the same name as them?!) showed us into an enormous sort of kitchen/living room/TV room. It was so lovely; there were two huge sofas in front of the biggest TV I've ever seen in my life. It was more like a cinema really. And at the other end of the room there was a massive dining table with a big vase of gorgeous flowers on it. The sort of flowers you see on the front of a magazine, like proper flowers – not a crummy bunch from a petrol station like the ones Dumbledore Chops brought Mum the other day. At Sam's it was all beautiful and perfect.

Sam's house reminded me a bit of some of the houses of the girls who I used to be at Greyfriars with. Even our old house never looked like that, even when we used to have more money! Mum's never been a swish-flowers-on-the-table type, I guess, unlike GB, who is definitely one of those, like Sam's mum. Only GB is a lot older, but just as snobby.

Samantha made tea and put out some absolutely yummy home-made flapjacks and Gran's cake that she'd sliced up. (I so wanted to eat loads of the flapjacks and the cake but managed not to!) We all sat around, and it was a bit eggy at first TBH. No one was saying much, even Gran who can usually talk for Britain, but then Sam, thank god, told us about how he'd been on a school trip (which is why I hadn't seen him walking Bonnie, I guess) and about how great it had been. And then Samantha asked where I was at school and when I said Heathside Academy, she definitely looked a bit embarrassed, because she paused for a moment and then replied, 'Oh, right. Good for you,' but like she meant the exact opposite.

Anyway, none of that was a big deal really compared to what happened later. I mean, anyone could have guessed, just from seeing the house and kitchen and everything, that Sam's mum was going to be a bit posh, but not that she'd be super horrible. Not all posh people are horrible – I should know!

After a bit, Gran and Sam's mum started talking about the puppies Bonnie was going to have and what was going to happen to them and all that.

Gran said, 'Well, I hear you're going to sell them and if that's the case I'd like to take them all, if that's okay with you.'

Sam's mum paused again (super annoying if she does that every time she speaks) and said, 'Ah, I see . . .' She said it in that way grown-ups say 'I see' when you just know what they really mean is they don't see at all but they're saying that because they don't like what you're saying.

And then Samantha said in a really snooty way, 'The thing is, each of these puppies, and there are going to be three, will sell for between seven and eight hundred pounds and . . .' She trailed off then and gave a sort of and-there-you-have-it wave of her hand, making it completely obvious that she realised Gran couldn't afford that kind of money.

I was so furious that she had just assumed that Gran wasn't as rich as she so obviously is. I didn't dare look at Sam in case he was doing an 'I agree with my mum' face.

Gran looked really shocked for a moment and then said, 'Well, the puppies are half mine anyway and since I gather you don't actually want them, and I do, it never occurred to me that money would come into it.'

Good for Gran. I was really proud of her. She was right as well. You can't not want something, complain about having it, but then want loads of money for it, can you?

Sam's mum gave Gran one of those 'oh dear, you don't understand' smiles, one of those smiles people do when they really want to sneer instead of smile. 'Ah, well, yes. I didn't want Bonnie to have puppies, that's right, but since she is and I've found out how much they go for it seemed silly not to take advantage of the situation.' And then she gave a little laugh as if that was going to make Gran suddenly see it all from her point of view.

I think that was probably what did it for Gran, who then said in a voice that was a mixture of sad and angry, 'I don't have that kind of money. If I did I'd happily pay for the puppies. But if I were in your situation I wouldn't dream of selling them. I'd just be delighted that someone was prepared to take them into a home where they were actually wanted.'

Which I thought was a really good point, because

wouldn't most dog lovers want at least some of the puppies from their own dog?

Then horrible Sam's mum let out another of those laughing-but-really-sneering little laughs and said, 'Ah, well, I'm clearly more of a hard-headed business-woman than you are!'

At that Gran stood up and said, 'Hard-*hearted* more like and clearly not a true dog-lover either. Tab, come on, we're leaving.'

I was a bit shocked and really embarrassed, but I did think Gran was right and I didn't think Sam's mum was being very nice at all, but still, it was pretty embarrassing having to suddenly stand up and march out like that.

Sam's mum sort of muttered a few things, which I didn't really hear. Something about the 'lovely cake', as if that would flatter Gran into forgetting everything.

I could see Sam out of the corner of my eye looking pretty awks, but I didn't say anything to him or even look at him. I was just so upset that Gran had been humiliated. And I could tell she was furious. Gran gathered Basil up and the three of us stomped out of the house. Well, I didn't stomp, Gran did, and Basil didn't stomp because he can't. I don't think dogs can stomp and anyway Gran was holding him.

Sam opened the front door for us and I could tell was trying to get me to look at him, but I wasn't going to no matter what he did or said. His mum had been rude to my gran and she didn't deserve it at all, and anyway it was only because she really, really loves dogs and would do anything for them. And that is not a reason to be rude to someone, ever.

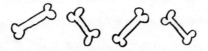

So that's it. We are not going to get the puppies. And Gran is really upset. And I'm never going to go out with Sam. Not that I want to now. I am never going to talk to him again. And Sam and I are never going to look cute walking our dogs and their puppies together. I hate him and his stuck-up mum. Oh god, what am I going to say if I bump into him when I walk Basil? Hmm, actually, that is not my problem, is it? It's Sam's. He's the one who should be super embarrassed. He's the one who should be worrying about what HE's going to say when he bumps into ME . . . I'll bet he isn't, though . . . I'll bet he doesn't care what I feel. I'll find a new place to walk Basil and I'll forget about Sam forever. Loser. (Him, not me BTW, obvs.)

AUTUMN TERM
WEEK 13

TUESDAY

So, you'll never guess what happened today when I was walking Basil.

'Tab! Tab! Taaaab!' I could hear someone, a boy, shouting my name. I didn't look round but knew it was Sam.

Or at least I was pretty sure it was. TBH a stranger, like a mad axeman or someone, wouldn't exactly call out your name if he was chasing you, would he? Anyway, durr, a crazy killer wouldn't know your name. I'd actually heard Sam the first time but I'd totes made my mind up long ago to completely ignore him if I ever did see him. I didn't care how many times he called out; I was not going to talk to him. That was final. I was never going to talk to him again. His mum had been so rude and snooty and snotty to my lovely gran and so completely 'all the puppies are mine' on top of being horrible and Sam had not said or done a single thing to try to make it all right.

If my mum had been like that to him or his mum, if they'd come over to ours, I'd definitely have said something to stop her or at least to let them know that I thought she was out of order. I'd never have just sat there with my mouth clamped shut like I thought her behaviour was completely fine. He's pathetic. He's a total mummy's boy and a loser and a drip, and I wanted nothing to do with him. My mind was made up.

But he didn't stop running after me or calling my name. He kept on going, even though I wouldn't stop, until eventually he caught up with me. When he finally reached me he was so out of breath he was really panting. He'd obviously been running fast. It was quite funny watching him bent over double trying to get his breath back.

'I don't want to talk to you, thanks very much, so

don't bother trying,' I said and walked on. Except I couldn't walk on, or actually march off, which is what I was planning to do, because Basil would not budge. It was like someone had nailed his paws into the ground. I tugged really hard and even yanked his lead (which he does not enjoy!) but he was like a huge heavy stone. No matter how hard I pulled I just could not move him. He was staring at Bonnie and she was staring back at him. They were like in a trance, literally locked together doing whatever the snogging equivalent is for dogs! (No tongues, though, obvs. YUCK and what a totes mankenstein idea!)

I tried not to catch Sam's eye. But it was hard because it was really funny and sweet; they were so totally thrilled to see each other. It had been weeks and Bonnie had obviously had her puppies, so they might have been talking to each other about that – oh god, I sound like Gran, but you know what I mean. Dog couples must def have a way of letting each other know they've given birth, don't you think?

I couldn't laugh or even smile, though, because I had to stay super angry in front of Sam. There was no way I was going to start letting him think that everything was okay. And then Basil, looking right into Bonnie's eyes, made a sort of whimpering sound and tilted his head to one side exactly the same way humans do when they're letting you know they feel sorry for you – it was uncanny.

Sam, who'd finally caught his breath, said, 'She's obviously just told him about the puppies. She had three, so he's a proud father now,' and then he looked at me and smiled and I couldn't help it, I smiled back.

Our two dogs were being so incredibly soppy and it did look like they were cooing over something special to only them. It was impossible not to smile. I was so cross. I did not mean to do that.

And then Sam, seeing me smile, obviously realising this was his in, started babbling really fast. I guess to make sure he got it all out before I walked off and he lost his chance.

'I'm so sorry about what happened. My mum felt

awful. She really didn't mean to be so rude and then I lost my phone the next day so I couldn't text or call you, and I've been walking Bonnie much more often than normal hoping I'd see you . . .'

I didn't know what to say at first, so I didn't say anything. I just shrugged my shoulders like I was saying 'whatevs'. I was actually thinking: Big deal. You're sorry, great, but nothing's really changed.

'Mum's been through a lot recently, my dad went off with his secretary, incredibly original, and they're now fighting over money and we might have to sell the house and . . . sorry, I'm not trying to give you the whole sob story, I'm just trying to explain why Mum was like that.'

Of course him saying that about his dad did make me feel sorry for him and I guess did sort of help me to understand why his mum had been so ghastly. After all, apart from the going-off-with-another-woman bit I have been through all that.

And then Sam, suddenly, literally out of nowhere, turned away, like to walk off, even though he'd only been there for a second. He just said, 'Well, that's all I wanted to say, so see you around,' and then he walked off!

Literally it was just like that. Completely amazeballs – one minute he's giving me a whole big apology and waffling on and then super abruptly he walks off as if his pants had caught fire. I was speechless. And I was furious that I'd smiled at him over our dogs. I should have stayed angry with him the whole time and never given him the chance to walk off like that, leaving me standing there like a lemon.

After he got a few steps away he turned round and said, 'Oh yes, I need your address. Mum would like to send your granny a note, you know, to apologise.'

He said it like it was something he'd nearly forgotten to ask and like it wasn't that big a deal anyway. So, great, even a note from his mum to Gran, which would mean so much to her, was like a 'who cares' for him. I was so surprised and actually a bit dumbstruck. I mean, he'd run after me like a maniac for ages, even after he must have realised I knew it was him and noticed that I wasn't stopping, so obvs I'd thought whatever he was running after me to say was going to turn out to be for a much bigger reason than just getting our address. It was so extra. All that effort, just for that, and it wasn't apparently even the main reason for running after me, which had been to explain his mum's behaviour.

I was really angry and I wanted to tell him to go away, but I knew Gran would be pleased with the note so I gave him our address and then just as I was about to properly flounce off, deliberately without saying goodbye or anything to make sure he knew I was super obviously Not Talking to Him, HE walked off! He managed to be the first to walk off. He just said 'cheers' and ran off doing a stupid little jog after Bonnie who had trotted ahead of him. HE WALKED OFF FIRST BEFORE I COULD SHOW HIM I WAS WALKING OFF!

Grrrr. Sam, who has not One Single Reason to be annoyed with me, walked off first, leaving me like I had meant him to feel – all eggy and awks and properly aware that he'd done something bad to me! He was the one supposed to be feeling uncomfortable and like he hadn't made it up with me, not the other way around! I could not believe what had happened. I was so cross. I had decided, if I ever did make it up with him, I'd be super frosty with him for ages and ages and make him really sweat and then only after he properly believed I was never going to talk to him again, then I'd maybe, maybe, start talking to him a bit. This had all gone wrong and so quickly I hadn't even had a chance to notice it was happening.

Also, the fact is, I have to admit, although I'm not going to tell anyone else – okay, maybe Grace, but that's it – I was a bit upset that he hadn't asked for my number again. (Which in my planned version of how things were going to go he was definitely going to do and he was going to have to ask like a zillion times, begging and pleading before I finally gave it to him.)

He said he'd lost his phone, which happens, right, so why didn't he ask for my number again? I guess I'd thought we were sort of making up, but I was obviously wrong. He doesn't care about me. He only wanted to talk to me so that he could get our address for his horrible mum. Great. I so wish I hadn't bumped into him after all. I was fine all that time I didn't talk to him or see him and now I'm cross and upset and feel like I let him get away with something . . . I don't know exactly what but, you know, I'd had my guard up really well and I've just let him break it down only to trot off without a care, at least about me, in the world. I AM ANNOYED.

AUTUMN TERM WEEK 11

TUESDAY (NOT THAT MUCH LATER)

I **heard the** front door knock, but didn't think anything about it. I knew it wasn't going to be for me. My mates and I all text each other first if we're planning on going to each other's houses. But then I heard Gran squealing, which I know probably sounds a bit random, maybe even a bit scary, but it's not that weird (or scary) if it's *my* gran doing the squealing. It would be if it was anyone else's gran because old ladies squealing is a bit . . . I dunno, extra, but Gran does do it quite a lot.

So this time, I just thought she'd got Basil into that

new jumpsuit she's been knitting him and was super thrilled with how he looked in it. (I am not kidding, it is literally a jumpsuit but with a special hole for him to wee through – major mankenstein. I swear to god I am NEVER EVER taking him out in that.)

Then Gran called up the stairs for me to come down. She sounded like it was really urgent. I didn't want to go down. I was in a super-bad mood because of what had just happened with Sam and didn't feel like pretending I thought Basil's latest outfit was fantastic.

Anyway, I'm never mean to Gran, so I did go down and guess what? You are never going to believe this. Sam was standing in the kitchen, in OUR KITCHEN, holding a basket with the sweetest little puppies you have ever seen in your life in it. There are the tiniest, teensiest things ever. They've got miniature black buttons for noses (not real buttons, durr, but that's what they look like) and their fur is soft and fluffy. They look like they've been blow-dried with a hair-dryer. They were peeping over the side of the basket, with their paws over the edge. It was just like a photo from the front of a tin of biscuits. TOTES ADORABLE.

Sam gave me a half-smile. 'Sorry I rushed off and didn't say anything, but I wanted to surprise you. Mum would like your gran to have these. Is that okay?' he said, turning to Gran.

'Okay? It's a great deal more than okay. It is just wonderful. I am thrilled. Please thank your mother very much!' Gran squeaked (she was so excited), holding out both her arms for the basket.

Sam handed it over and Gran plonked herself down in her chair, lowering the basket onto her lap. She was literally in heaven – puppy heaven! She started making baby noises at the puppies, which was a bit embarrassing in front of Sam, natch.

I was super pleased for Gran, and, yes, all right, really pleased that Sam had gone to all that effort to surprise me, but obvs I was also panicking that Sam was in our house – aaaargh. Sam was actually inside my house! It was major.

You could fit about two million of our houses into

his house. We didn't have any posh flowers on the kitchen table (as if, we never do). It was just like our house always is – messy, not done up and chaotic. And also I was panicking about what if Luke walked in or, worse, Mum, or, total disaster, Dumbledore Chops popped round (like he is always doing these days – I don't know why he doesn't just move in he's here so often). Erm, there was no way I was going to let *him* meet Sam. He would so show me up with his look-at-me-understanding-kids-today non-stop head nodding. So, I wanted to get Sam out of my house as quickly as possible to avoid anything like that but obvs I didn't want to look like I was still cross with him.

I was definitely NOT cross with him any more. I immediately realised that he'd been all casual and 'got to run off now' back then on purpose, so I wouldn't cotton on to what he was planning. That was soooooo sweet. But I didn't know what to do. I wanted to have time with Sam talking about it and thanking him but not in my house and not in front of my gran.

I managed to say, 'Thanks very much,' and smiled at him.

And then, thank god, Sam said he had to go (but not in a 'who cares' way at all this time) and Gran said, 'Thank you so much. Please tell your mother how grateful I am and how much it means to me.'

And then she handed something over to him. At first I couldn't see what it was, but as Sam looked at them I could see it was the tiniest little pair of knitted baby booties and a baby's bonnet.

'Thinking I was going to get the puppies a while back I knitted these for them, so that's a set for the puppy you and your mother have kept,' Gran explained to Sam, who was looking at them like he couldn't work out what they were and that whatever they were they were way extra.

I thought they were adorable, even if they were for a dog. But I must admit if you're not used to your granny knitting endless amounts of wacky outfits for your dog then it might seem a bit crazy.

Then Gran looked over at me and said, 'Tabitha, please see Sam out,' which was fantastic because it gave me an excuse to take him to the front door and not be with him in front of Gran, which I was finding more and more embarrassing, especially seeing as he was now holding miniature booties and a bonnet like they were bags of stinky poo! He obviously did not want to be seen carrying them home!

Gran asking me to see him out meant I didn't have to look like it was my idea to take him to the door because I was sooo keen. This way I was taking him to the front door because my gran had told me to, super-caj. Just as he walked down the path away from our house Sam turned round and said, 'Oh yes, can I get your number again, you know, because I lost my phone?'

I managed to keep my cool and gave it to him but as soon as I closed the door I just could not help it: I broke into a sort of mad crazy dance around the hall shouting, 'Yes! Yes! Yes!' and waving my arms around in the air. I was soooooo incredibly pleased he'd asked for it again because that must mean he really, actually wants my number now because he can't even say it's about arranging for Gran to see the puppies or anything like that. There is no excuse for him to have it except that he wants it. Sam wants my phone number! Oh yes! He has asked for my number officially and that is definite. FANTASTIC.

What a great day! The only bad thing was that I was still doing my little dance of happiness when Luke walked in through the front door. He gave me a really long look, raised his eyebrows and said super sarky, 'Smooth moves,' but I didn't care. I was floating on air and I did not, do not and never will care what that little squirt thinks of me or my dancing! And then I had a brainwave. I knew this was my chance at last. I kept dancing and said to him, 'One does not care what you, you little squirt, thinks of one.'

Oh man, you should have seen his face! Luke was amazed. I outwitted him for probably the first time in my life. Well, with swotty language stuff, that is. He could not believe it. This might end up being the best day of my life!

AUTUMN TERM
WEEK 11

WEDNESDAY

I **could not** wait to get to school today. I couldn't wait to tell my gang about Sam and the puppies and him asking for my number again and the whole coming over with the basket surprise . . . everything. It was all soooooo exciting.

And the puppies are just the sweeeeeetest things in the entire world. Even Mum went all gooey when she saw them. She seemed to completely forget about her total meltdown when she said we couldn't cope with two more dogs. When she came in the puppies were curled up asleep together in the basket Sam had brought them over in like tiny commas.

Mum had peered in and broken into a huge smile. 'Are these the famous grandchildren, then, Mum?' she asked Gran. I instantly knew that if she was calling them that she was letting Gran know she wasn't going to kick up a fuss about them living with us.

Gran had nodded back and said, 'Full house, eh?' to Mum and then they'd had a little hug and both had tears in their eyes. What is it with grown-ups and crying? Mum and Gran tear up at practically everything and usually it's not even sad stuff. Extra and random or what?!

Actually, I have to admit it was quite nice seeing them like that with each other for a change, because Gran does wind Mum up quite a lot, especially with all the Basil-is-my-son-and-therefore-your-brother-too stuff she insists on doing. But, you know what, I have to admit Mum has become a bit more chilled these days. Don't know why, but she's def a bit less stressy and she doesn't do so much nagging about what I'm eating or how fat she thinks I'm getting, which is really great too. Thinking about it, she's even stopped going on and on about how I don't read and she def doesn't know that I'm reading in secret . . . unless she's been poking about in my room, which I sort of doubt, because annoying as Mum can most def be, she isn't that kind of nosey. Anyway, I usually lock my room. I mean, there is no point in having the only room in the house with a door that locks if you don't lock it, is there? You know what they say: use it or lose it.

I'd taken a pic on my phone of the puppies to show everyone at school – well, actually I'd taken about a million – and I showed my lot during break. (Even I'm not daring enough to get my phone out in class. There's this new rule that if a teacher catches you with your phone in class they can take it off you for a whole week. A whole week? How extra is that? No one can do without their phone for a whole week so it's a good rule, I guess, if you're a teacher.)

Emz, A'isha and Grace squealed with delight over the photos. They were all trying to grab my phone so they could get a better look. Everyone was so desperate to see them in the end I invited them all back to mine after school. I know I don't usually and I know I've said it's a bit risky – Luke being weird, Gran talking for Basil, Mum being . . . well, Mum-ish, and Dumbledore Chops being, well, just there – but I so wanted them all to see the puppies in real life and anyway I can't not have my bezzies round for the rest of my life just in case my weird family weirds them out, can I? Sometimes you've just got to get on with it, haven't you? Anyway, I bet everyone in the world thinks their family is weirder than everyone else's, don't you think?

On the way home I gave everyone all the details, about how Sam had chased me and then tricked me into thinking he only wanted my address for the note from his mum to Gran and him bringing the puppies round and asking for my phone number again and everything.

'Oh man, that is way extra. It's so romantic. You two are def going to get married,' A'isha said.

We all laughed except Grace who, after obviously thinking about it for a bit, said super seriously, 'I think you'd have to know each other considerably longer before contemplating such a big step.'

Honestly, Grace is weird sometimes. She can't really have thought A'isha was serious.

Everyone made faces at her and I replied, 'Yes, one would do certainly have to do that,' and everyone cracked up, even Grace. No one has ever let her forget that time she said 'one' instead of 'you'. It was so extra. But it did give me that chance to use it against Luke and it totally aced him.

'Even so, he must be super keen, Tab,' Emz said after a bit, just before we got to mine.

I didn't know what to say. I hope he is. But I don't want to be too keen back — not because I'm not interested but because I don't really want to be thinking about him all the time and get all stressy about when and if he's going to ring, and when we'll meet and what we'd do if we did meet. You know, that couples stuff. I sort of want to know he likes me, def, but I'm not completely sure I want to start seriously dating or anything major like that. Don't get me wrong, I do really like him but right now I more like knowing he's asked for my number and that he's sort of 'there', if that makes sense, you know?

♡FRIENDS♡

As soon as we all got in the door at my house everyone rushed towards the basket the puppies were in. It's so cute. They go back in there as soon as they've finished having a little play with Basil or Gran. Actually Basil's not really playing with them. He really is being like a dad (well, not my dad obvs, but a Regular Dad) – he's watching them and sitting quietly near them, to protect them, I guess, and he's not doing any of his normal jigging about near them either.

Mum and Gran were in, but that was okay, and get this, as soon as we all plonked ourselves down on the floor to play with the puppies, Mum brought out a plate of biscuits – really nice ones, like the-kind-that-are-so-nice-I've-never-seen-them-in-our-house-before that's how nice (what is up with Mum?!) – and gave them to us. Just like that. Like it's the most normal thing in the world for Mum to be chilled about me eating biscuits!

It was soooo nice. I was so relieved. It was like I was being rewarded for finally bringing my mates back to ours. It was brilliant. I could tell all my bezzies were fine with being there, even when Luke came in and said something completely mankenstein about rescuing two snails he'd found on the pavement. Yuck, who cares? But no one seemed to notice how weird and pathetic he is, which is just great.

After a while – it was ages, actually . . . Honestly you (or should that be one?) would play with those puppies all day long if you got the chance. It's like the best thing in the whole wide world. Anyway, Gran invited everyone to stay for supper. Oh god. She hadn't asked me first, so for a moment I wanted to die in case no one said yes, but it was fine because all three of them said they would! Result.

I quickly checked that Gran wasn't doing one of her throw-everything-in-a-pot suppers, which are okay, if you're us, because we're used to them, but for new people, especially my bezzies having supper at ours for the first time ever, would be a bit, well, I don't want to be mean, but truthfully mankenstein. But, fantastic news, she was doing one of her best – lasagne – and I was fine with that, and so was everyone.

And then, get this, you are not going to believe it, well, actually, I suppose you are, because maybe it has been a bit obvs, but I haven't wanted to think about it, Mum said she was going out. I was like, 'But it's supper time, where are you going?' and then Mum looked at Gran and Gran gave her a little 'it's all right' face and then Mum looked at me and then at Luke and then at the floor for a second.

Then she said, 'I'm going out with Frank, erm, for supper . . .'

And before I could even think it Luke blurted out, 'What, like on a date?'

Mum smiled and said, 'Yes, a date. We are, I guess you'd say, dating.'

Well, there is no way I was going to let this ruin

having my bezzies over and it going well so far, and anyway I wasn't even that interested so I just said, 'Yeah, whatevs,' to show that I didn't want her to start talking about all that stuff in front of my mates. I saw Mum look at Gran and raise her eyebrows, but it's fine. I am actually not that bothered, as long as they don't start doing all yucky lovey-dovey stuff round at ours I don't care. And if it means Mum's more chilled and buys nice biscuits then great.

AUTUMN TERM
WEEK 11

WEDNESDAY (LATER)

After everyone had gone and I was in my room getting ready for bed, Luke put his head round the door.

'I guess Mum and Dad will get a divorce then.'

I knew he'd thought that the moment Mum had made her Big Dating Announcement, if that's what it was.

TBH I suppose I had thought that too but I just shrugged my shoulders. I didn't know what to say. I really don't want to think about all that. It's too epic and real.

'I'm not going to stop calling him Dumbledore Chops, though, no matter what,' Luke said as he left.

'Yeah, me neither!' I called after him.

DUMBLEDORE
CHOPS
← NOT A COOL
BEARD

It was really, really great having all my mates round and supper had been properly nice and they all loved playing with the puppies. I just wish that was all I had to think about. Like a normal thirteen-year-old girl. I'll bet normal girls get to think about their mates, boys, maybe a bit of school stuff and having fun and that's it.

I just wish I didn't have this other news to think about too. Because of course I started thinking about what Dad was going to say when he found out. Not that he's got much of a leg to stand on, but you know what I mean. And then what if he gets a girlfriend? And then about if things will be different if Mum and Dad are actually divorced. And, oh god, what if Mum marries Dumbledore Chops . . . And GB already wants me to go and live there, and what if Mum and Dumbledore Chops send me anyway? Oh man, sometimes there is way too much different stuff to have to think about, isn't there?

'I **can't believe** she's accepted my offer!' Gran exclaimed.

She was reading a letter that had just arrived in the post. And then she started laughing, 'I cannot believe it. The woman is a one-off. Just incredible!'

I didn't know what she was talking about, obvs. TBH I wasn't that interested either. I was actually trying to do some homework. Yeah, homework, me, would you believe?! I know, random or what? The thing is, and so far only Grace knows about this, I am actually finding the sociology bit of ESC really interesting – it's all about how and why people behave in certain ways and how much outside stuff, like where they live and how poor or rich they are, makes them behave like that. Something in all that made me think about Dad and his drinking, and all that spoiling everything, even though to start with he had much more than lots and lots of people do. Don't get me wrong, I'm not about to turn into a major swot or head prefect or anything like that!

Grace made me laugh my head off when I told her about this. She said, 'It's because you're engaged with the subject.'

'Engaged with the subject'?? Yeah, like I love it so much I'm going to marry it! I think she means I find it interesting, which is true, I suppose.

It's nice having someone like Grace to tell things like that to because she is never ever sarky no matter what I tell her, and although I totes love Emz and A'isha of course, I'm pretty sure they'd have thought I was joking if I'd told them about suddenly being interested in the stuff we're learning. They'd have been all, 'Oh yeah, right, we get it. You're pretending to be interested in this because you're cooking up something hilarious. Can't wait to see what it is,' and then it would have been tricky trying to tell them I actually wasn't.

And then they might have been disappointed with me for not doing what I usually do. It's weird because when I started at HAC I really, really, more than anything in the world, wanted to be the funniest, rudest, most popular girl in the class, and I still do, but sometimes when I don't feel like making a super-big effort to keep it all going I have to do it anyway because I know everyone's expecting me to. It's kind of like I've started something that is easy for me most of the time, so that's fine, but which I have to keep doing even when it's not easy because that's what everyone now expects. Does that make sense? But I don't want to stop doing it only to find out no one likes me as much – way too risky. Anyway, I'm not planning on stopping being cheeky. I'm just saying it's hard to do ALL the time! Oh man, that sounds so complicated, stress-y and way too think-y. I've got to chill out! But anyway, that is why I'm only telling Grace.

I was doing this homework at the kitchen table, even though I've got a table in my room. I hate being on my own most of the time anyway, but especially doing homework and anyway Mum wasn't in to nag me to do it upstairs. So, Gran was so excited by whatever was in that letter she picked Basil up and literally danced around the kitchen holding him with her arms outstretched like he was a proper dancing partner! I don't think Basil loved it.

Then Gran caught my eye and yelped, 'Oh my word! What was I thinking of?! You should be the first to know! This –' she waved the letter –'is from your other granny, GB as you like to call her. She's going to stop all that custody nonsense and take one of the pups instead of you! Isn't that marvellous?!'

I stared at Gran for a bit trying to understand what she was saying. Gran was going to give away one of her adored 'grandchildren', Basil's puppies, just to keep me? GB would rather have a dog than me and Gran would rather have me than a dog? I burst into tears. It was all so weird and random and . . . I didn't understand anything.

Gran came rushing over, sat down in the chair next to mine and pulled me onto her lap. It would have been funny if I hadn't been crying. I'm taller than Gran is now!

'You can't give up one of your pups,' I sobbed. 'You wanted them so much! You adore them!'

Gran hugged and shushed me. 'I do adore them but nothing like as much as I adore you. Oh, stop crying, my darling,' she went on very gently and nicely. 'If GB is silly enough to accept a puppy over you then I think I've got a very good deal,' which did make me smile. Then Gran dropped her voice to a whisper and said, 'Don't tell him, but I'd even give Basil away before I ever agreed to give you away.'

Basil happened to squeak at that same exact moment, which of course was a coincidence, but Gran winked at me, turned to him and said, 'Don't worry, darling, I was talking about another Basil!' which made me laugh out loud and really cheered me up.

Gran made me some hot chocolate and told me everything. I'd known about that first letter GB had written suggesting I live with her and go back to Greyfriars obvs, but after telling my bezzies and having a laugh about it I hadn't thought about it much since, because even if Mum and Gran had thought it was a good idea, which I already knew they didn't, there was no way I was going to go or anyone was going to make me go.

But then Gran told me that GB had got angry after Mum had refused and had got a lawyer – a lawyer! I did think that was a bit extra. And the lawyer's letter had said GB and Dad wanted joint custody of me, which apparently would have meant me spending term time, i.e. at Greyfriars, with them and the rest of the time here at Gran's. OMG.

I could not believe what Gran was telling me. 'Your poor mum was so worried, and so was I, that they might win, and we couldn't afford a lawyer, so it was all a bit nerve-wracking for a bit. And then

Frank stepped in and sorted it all out. He's been a big help.'

Hmm, might have known Dumbledore Chops had got involved. He's always around these days. Obvs I was glad he'd helped them but, honestly, he's always sticking his nose into our stuff! It's not like he's part of our family or anything. He's just an old pal of Gran's. Okay, I realise that he is a bit more than that now to Mum, but, yuck, I do not want to think about that! Mankenstein.

The fact that she's calling him – bleurgh, pukarama – her actual boyfriend – pass the sick bucket – is bad enough. Urgh. Don't want to think about it. But apparently, Gran explained, Frank had found out what GB could and couldn't do and, basics, had helped them write her a letter telling her she had 'no claim to custodial rights', whatever that means. It had been Gran's idea to offer one of the pups to get GB to drop the idea completely and to stop her writing back again demanding this, that and the other.

Gran telling me that nearly made me cry again. It did seem a bit weird, though, that GB would go to all that effort and then just give up for a puppy. Gran explained that she wasn't really giving up for that reason, but because she couldn't do it all legally she'd decided if she offered GB the pup it would give her a way of feeling like she had actually won . . . at least a bit. Gran reckoned the whole thing was really about GB wanting to get one over Mum – pathetic, eh? GB is ancient, and Dad is a grown-up (well, sort of!) and she's still trying to make sure he wins everything. Oh man, if Mum is like that with Luke when he's grown up I'll go berserk! Apparently it was ridiculous to start with because only Dad could 'legally apply for joint custody' Gran said, not his mum, and we all know Dad can barely get it together to apply for a library card, never mind one of his kids!

When I told my gang they literally could not believe it. Everyone decided GB is a complete witch. And I agree. I hate her for doing this in the first place and I hate her even more for taking one of the pups. And do you know what's random? I hate her a bit too for agreeing to take a dog instead of me. I know I never wanted to go, but you'd think if she really loved me she'd keep fighting for me. I know I shouldn't be saying that because I do not want to live with her but, you know, this proves that she doesn't love me or Luke anything like as much as Gran does.

One good thing is at least when (maybe that should be 'if' now!) we go down to visit Dad we'll have a dog to play with, which will be way better than being made to go out for long walks with GB or having to sit around listening to her go on about how nothing is ever Dad's fault and how marvellous he is. Incredible but true — that is still what GB thinks about him! And I suppose, this way, Dad's got a new dog, so maybe he won't mind about Mum having a . . . oh man, I can hardly bear to say it . . . okay, here goes . . . gulp, boyfriend. There, I've said it. Yuckarama, though.

AUTUMN TERM
WEEK 12

THURSDAY (LATER)

I'm just about to go to sleep. Got Muzzy tucked up with me — sort of felt like I really wanted her with me tonight. Which is SO not a big deal. I can't believe the whole GB-trying-to-get-me thing went so far and got so serious and all the while I didn't know anything about it. It's really not like Mum not to have gone on and on and on about it, moaning about it all day long. Usually she makes such a huge big deal out of the smallest thing. I guess that means she must actually have been really worried, so I suppose it's good then that Dumbledore Chops helped her. I don't like to think of Mum being worried and upset, especially not by Dad's mum — honestly, as per usual, GB was doing Dad's dirty work for him! Huh, Mum might as well have never bothered to marry Dad; she should have just married GB!

Honestly, the whole thing about asking for just me and not Luke was so extra of GB. Hmm, can't work out if that means I can torture Luke with that info or not, because it's not like either of us love her like we love Gran. Still, thinking about it, I'm sure I can use it to wind Luke up in some way . . . It's got to be good ammunition . . . Yeah, and perhaps I can use 'one' too . . . BRILLIANT idea!

Piccadilly
PRESS

Thank you for choosing a Piccadilly Press book.

If you would like to know more about our authors, our books or if you'd just like to know what we're up to, you can find us online.

www.piccadillypress.co.uk

You can also find us on:

We hope to see you soon!